BILLIONAIRE COWBOY'S WEDDING CRASHER

Billionaire Cowboys of True Love, Texas,
Book Two

HOPE
MOORE

Billionaire Cowboy's Wedding Crasher

Copyright © 2020 Hope Moore

This book is a work of fiction. Names and characters are of the author's imagination or are used fictitiously. Any resemblance to an actual person, living or dead, is entirely coincidental.

Billionaire Cowboy's Wedding Crasher

When confirmed billionaire bachelor, Levi Tanner catches the garter at his brother's wedding he's not happy. Especially since his brother caught a garter at their friend's wedding and now he's just married his one true-love...or so Cole keeps telling him. And now his brother is all smiles that Levi's caught the garter and telling him he better get ready because his bachelor status might just be about to change. And then he spots a woman sneaking pictures of the wedding and now he's caught a wedding crasher. If there is one thing the Tanner brothers don't like its snoopy reporters. And this one is about to find out she's not welcome at the wedding.

When Rita Snow comes face to face with the most gorgeous Tanner brother of them all her heart is pounding. When he accuses her of being a wedding crasher out to sell her photos to the highest bidder. He doesn't know how much she needs the money these photos will bring or how much she hates the sleaziness of what she's doing. Will Levi understand? Can she trust him with her secret?

When these billionaire cowboys each catch a wedding garter, the next woman they meet is their one true-love. Sounds simple.

Not so fast…

This is a smile worthy clean & wholesome romance series you'll love.

PROLOGUE

Previously at the end of Billionaire Cowboy's Runaway Bride…

Levi Tanner watched his brother Cole dancing with his soulmate, Tulip. The wedding had been attended by a large number of friends and family here at the main ranch, among the beautiful landscaping that Tulip had done. Levi stood near the outer edge of the dance floor, observing, like he liked to do. And at the table on the other side of the huge turquoise ceramic pot of flowers was the table where Tulip's mother and some of her friends were sitting and enjoying themselves.

"That Tulip Michelle is just the most beautiful bride I have ever seen, Mira."

"Why, thank you, Beulah Anne. I was thinking the very same thing. If any of those horrible tabloid people are here, she will take all their readers' breath away in that dress. And my new son-in-law isn't shabby himself. Those Tanner men do have the looks, don't they?"

"You are right about that. You are going to have some gorgeous grandbabies." Beulah Anne cocked her blue-haired head and met Levi's gaze that had momentarily drifted to the ladies' table. She smiled. "That Levi is a showstopper, that one."

She winked at him; he tipped his head and then immediately put his gaze somewhere else.

Tabloids. The mere mention of the creepy reporters who liked to stalk them had him surveying the wedding-goers. They'd backed off Tulip and Cole after the flashy show Tulip had put on for them that night she'd said to heck with them and proposed to Cole at the gate, in full view of God and everyone. The videos had trended online as the Runaway Bride Gets Her Man and she had succeeded in turning the tide on the bad news that Shelly had tried to bury them under.

Tulip's business had flourished after the proposal went viral. And, all in all, the world was all rosy for them, though she swore that soon they would be able to settle down and have a normal life because she and Cole were going to be blissfully happy and to tabloids that was really boring.

He thought she was living in a dream world, because the tabloids weren't known for letting go of a good thing. And Tulip had turned out to be a reader magnet. She and Cole together, being all smoochy, smoochy gave them heart palpitations. Levi was happy for his brother, he really was, but the media was not something he would ever embrace.

His thoughts hit a snag as his gaze landed on a beautiful brunette with a shapely figure and her startlingly blue eyes slammed into him. He felt as if he'd been burned by a blue flame. Their gazes collided, tangled, and then she turned and mixed into the crowd on the other side of the dance floor. He just stood there, stunned, feeling as though his world had just collided with a meteorite.

He moved from his position on the outskirts of the

party into the throng as the music to the bride and groom's dance neared the end. He searched, feeling almost frantic to catch a glimpse of her before something happened and she disappeared out of his life forever. Several people called his name; he nodded but kept moving.

Beck McCoy from Stonewall, another happily married man of recent days, called his name and tipped his hat. They often used Beck's Learjet charter service to travel these days as commercial flights were harder and harder to deal with. Bret had flown in from his bull-riding event using McCoy Charters just so he could get to the wedding on time, and he'd fly out later tonight in order to be back for tomorrow's nationally televised event.

"You look like you're looking for a woman," Beck said, not holding him up.

"Yeah, about five foot four or five, brunette, with amazing eyes. Did you see her pass by here?"

Beck's lip hitched upward. "Can't say that I did. But then, I had my eyes on that sweet little blue-eyed blonde." He nodded toward his wife, who danced on the edge of the floor with a small girl. They were laughing and happy, and he could see why Beck didn't see anyone in the room but his wife.

Just then, he saw her. A camera lifted in her hand as she snapped several shots of Cole dipping Tulip to the end of the wedding song and then planting a long, deeply involved kiss on his bride.

The blue-eyed beauty kept snapping photos—not like a normal partygoer would take a few; this woman was taking them consecutively, wanting the perfect shot. The money shot.

And then he knew, without doubt, that this was no guest. This was one of them, the photo jerks who crashed weddings of the wealthy, famous, or otherwise sought-after by the media for pictures to post. Paparazzi, photo opportunist looking for their money shot to make a paycheck. He and his brothers called them Paparats most of the time, like the rats they were.

This wedding list had been meticulously cleaned to make certain no paparats would get in.

But here she was, and he planned to take those

photographs off her hands. Striding forward, he neared her just as she spotted him. Looking guilty as sin, she backed up, pocketed the small camera, and took off through the crowd.

And he was in hot pursuit. She was not getting off the property with that camera.

CHAPTER ONE

Levi was in a hurry to catch the beautiful woman he had spotted taking pictures, not just any pictures, but what he had suspected were pictures of his brother's wedding that she planned to sell. People who were selling photos just had a look about them, and though this woman was beautiful, she had been taking too many pictures of Cole and Tulip to be for her own personal use and she was not the official photographer.

"Hold up, Levi," Cole called as he was preparing to toss the garter he had just removed from Tulip's leg.

Levi didn't need to be in the lineup for the garter

catching because he had no plans to be marrying anytime soon, so he'd leave that to all those guys standing there waiting.

But Cole pointed to the lineup. "Get in line."

"That's okay. I've got to get somewhere."

Cole laughed, the joy in his expression completely filling the entire room. "Yeah, in the lineup to catch this garter. Now get in line. You can go wherever you've got to go after this but come on, bro—line up."

Better get it over with; the sooner he could do that, the sooner he could maybe catch the brunette. "Fine, throw that thing."

Cole laughed and the guys standing around Levi nudged him, acting as if they didn't want him to be in the front of the line and they certainly didn't want him to get the garter.

He backed up a little bit. "Have at it, fellas. I don't want anything to do with it."

His older brother Austin, the doctor in the family, gave him a sidelong look. "I'm not particularly happy about being in this lineup either, but it's for Cole."

"Yeah, and he swears by that old wives' tale that

if you catch the garter, you're next in line to get married since he got hit in the face with the garter at the last wedding he went to and then met Tulip."

"That doesn't mean it's real."

"You've got that right. Whether I caught a garter or didn't, I'm not getting married. But no sense tempting fate." He grinned at Austin.

Cole turned his back to them and flung the garter over his head. It flew through the air and all the guys rushed for it like linebackers headed toward a quarterback. Only problem was one of them was overzealous and tripped. And they all went down right in front of Levi and Austin in a major pileup.

The garter sailed straight at Levi and slammed him in the chest. In reaction—a complete reflex—he snatched the garter before it landed on the ground and he stood there, gaping at it.

Austin laughed. "Look at you."

He glared. "This is ridiculous."

* * *

Rita Snow snapped photos of the billionaire Cole

Tanner and his new bride, Tulip. Her fingers trembled as she held the camera and she hoped no one noticed she hadn't been invited to this wedding but instead was a wedding crasher, here for the photos.

This was the wedding of the summer. The first of the Tanner brothers was getting married. They were overnight billionaire cowboys and the most eligible bachelors in the Hill Country area right now. This was a big, sought-after event. And she had crashed the wedding in order to get these photos.

Her stomach rolled back and forth just thinking about what she was doing. Looking over her shoulder, she hoped no one realized her camera was a powerful professional grade camera or that she was taking far more photos than any regular wedding guest would take. A light sheen of perspiration pebbled across her forehead as she snapped another shot of the groom preparing to throw the garter. Levi Tanner had noticed her earlier; she'd gotten away from him but she didn't want him to spot her again. She could still feel the electricity that had arced between them only moments earlier when their gazes had locked. She felt a little faint thinking about the intensity of Levi's gorgeous eyes as they caught hers. And then they'd narrowed, and she realized he knew…or was suspicious. He was the brother, it was said, who had no patience whatsoever for paparazzi. Not that she was calling herself that. She was just here to take some photos to sell. *Then why do I feel so sleazy?*

She had quickly hurried into the crowd, who at that time was gathered around, watching the bride and groom dancing together. She had panicked as she had rushed through the crowd and been thankful that she wasn't all that tall and could blend in. She had found a large palm plant to sink into the shadows behind and had waited for Levi to pass by as he searched for her.

She managed to get near the door and was about to make her escape when she had heard Cole call Levi's name and tell him to get in the garter lineup. He'd responded, teasing his brother about not getting in the line. But when she saw him get in line to catch the garter, she could not turn away.

She had hurried back to the edge of the crowd, slipped in front of the line, again glad she was smaller, and was now waiting in the front row to get her shot. If there was anything other than the picture of the happy couple that could bring money, it would be of the other brothers, who were now the most eligible bachelors in Texas. If one of them caught the garter, that could bring a great price tag.

Watching Levi, reluctant but at least standing there, she was thrilled at the amazing shots she got of the pileup on the floor in front of him and his brother, and the perfect shot she got of the garter hitting him in the chest and his reflex catch. Surprise had been written all over his handsome face when he looked down and realized he was holding the garter. She thought his expression was priceless, and hopefully a tabloid would think so, too, and pay her a nice sum.

She was smiling, mesmerized by the man. Only when his shocked gaze found hers did she realize she had let her guard down. His gaze locked onto hers and she saw instant recognition. She froze in place until she saw him slap the garter into his brother Austin's hands and start her way.

She spun and dove between the couple behind her.

Moving fast, she wove her way through the crowd toward the exit. No time to hide. It was time to leave. This cowboy knew exactly what she was doing, and he was coming for her.

She made it out the door and hurried down the path of the wedding venue, with its lighted lanterns and miles and miles of white tulle and lace that was tied along the walkway. Hanging on to her camera, she fumbled with the cover on the side, protecting the memory card. She stumbled as she got it open and managed not to fall, which was a miracle in the heels she was wearing. She glanced over her shoulder in time to see the door opening and Levi emerge.

She rushed forward into the parking lot and ejected the memory card. She had to hide it in case he caught her and took her camera. The only place that might be was in her bra. She yanked her neckline out and rammed it into her bra and breathed a sigh of relief that it was safe, secure against her thundering heart.

Breathing hard, she dove behind a car then hunched down and began weaving through the cars. When she was far enough away, she slammed her back against the fender of a truck and peered over the hood just as he was passing by. He was about fifteen feet away, with his back to her. Her breath whooshed out of her. If he turned, she was toast. Practically crab-crawling, she hurried to the next row and then made a mad dash for her car.

This was not going to end well if he caught her. She had to get these photos to her computer. Relief swept through her as she reached her compact rental car. She was thankful she'd had the vision to not lock it, just in case she needed to make a fast getaway. She had the key on a rubber wrist band and fumbled as she took the band off and rammed the key into the ignition. Seconds later, she had the car started and backed out. She didn't know where Levi was but she hoped he was still far enough away that she could drive across the grass to the road leading out onto the country road in front of the wedding venue. Hill Country was riddled with wedding venues across the hundreds of winding roads.

She had just started toward the grassy section she was going to use as a shortcut to freedom when he raced from between the cars, arms waving. And stood right in her path!

"Get out of the way," she shouted inside the car, but he stood his ground.

Fearful she would hit him, she yanked the steering wheel, lost control, and screamed as the car smashed straight into a small pond in the middle of the grassy section.

Screaming and furious, she tried to push the door open, but it wouldn't open. Steam poured from under the hood, as if the car were on fire. Panic seized her and she pushed on the door again, while water began to pool at her feet.

* * *

Levi ran toward the steaming car, madder than he could remember being in a very long time. *Fool woman hadn't stopped!* He wasn't panicking over the smoke, knowing that was from the engine hitting the water and would die off soon. But she'd almost ran over him.

Just went to show you that these types would do anything for a picture. Even risk his life or their life or anybody's life who came in the way of them getting their money shot.

Growling, he raced into the thigh-high water and yanked on the door handle. It didn't come open, so he yanked harder. She looked panicked inside, probably terrified of the smoke.

"Hang on," he yelled and yanked on the door again. This time, it came open and water poured into the interior of the car, chest high in the low-riding car. He reached for her as she reached for him, and he pulled her from the car. "Come with me. What were you thinkin'?" he growled as he half dragged her toward the shore. The camera was still dangling from around her neck.

"You jumped in front of me," she sputtered.

"And you could've died, or you could've killed me."

"Why did you do that?" she gasped, stumbling as they reached the muddy bank.

Not being very delicate, he let her fall to the

ground. He was normally not a bad guy, but this was just ridiculous. "There, you're safe. Now hand me that camera."

Breathing hard and on her knees, she glared up at him. "Why did you get in front of me like that? You caused this."

He didn't wait on her to hand him the camera; he reached down and pulled it from around her neck. "You were taking unauthorized pictures. I know your type. These are for money."

"It's not what you think."

"Oh yeah, right. I don't know how you're getting home tonight but you're not taking this camera with you."

A golf cart filled with two very broad-shouldered and completely stereotypical bodyguards raced across the grass and came to a stop. Both of them barreled out of the golf cart. "You have trouble, Mr. Tanner?" one of them asked.

The other one hurried to the water's edge near the woman. "Nobody else is in there, are they?"

"No." Her voice cracked.

"I believe it's just her, from what she says." He felt guilty that he hadn't asked that question. But the woman had been at the dance; surely, she hadn't left anyone in the car waiting on her. Still, he felt a niggling of guilt for not having asked the question. Or having looked inside for someone else.

"So, what's going on? Is everything okay?"

"This is a wedding crasher. I don't know how she got in. But I do know how she's getting out. Please take her away and either call a taxi or take her wherever she needs to go. Just get her out of here."

He held the camera up and then, giving her one last glare and being hit equally hard with a glare from those beautiful eyes of hers, he turned with the camera in his hand and strode across the grass, back toward the wedding. He'd had it with people invading his and his family's privacy.

CHAPTER TWO

R ita walked into her hotel room, wet, filthy, and feeling very grungy after her disastrous encounter with Levi at the Tanner wedding. She felt the slimy sense of what she had done, and she wanted to cry. Instead, she locked the door, walked into the tiny bathroom, and turned on the hot water. She pulled the memory card from her bra and stared at it. She felt nauseous looking at it. Unsure what to do with it, she went to the bedroom and slipped the small black card beneath the mattress. She had until eleven to get the pictures into her contact at the tabloid.

She was selling someone's private moments to a tabloid.

Feeling like a slime ball, she stripped off her

soaked clothes and let them fall to the ground. She had time for a shower, desperately needed a shower.

Time to think about this.

She stared at herself in the mirror. This was a disaster. But she needed the money these photos would bring. Shaking her head, she climbed into the shower and tried to wash away the dirty feelings assaulting her.

She could not let this opportunity pass her by.

The steaming hot water hit her, and she closed her eyes and let it wash over her. She stood there for a long time, just letting the hot water wash away how dirty she felt.

She'd had to talk herself into going through with this in the first place. And it had been hard to convince her to go against everything she believed in and invade someone's privacy. She told herself she had to do it, but it made her skin crawl. And obviously she was bad at it.

Not the actual picture taking—she had some fantastic pictures on the memory card. Pictures she knew were going to be wonderful. She knew how to take photos, just not how to not have a guilty conscience and feel like scum selling them.

She stayed in the shower for a long time, trying to talk herself into uploading the pictures and sending them into her contact. Finally, she climbed from the steaming shower, feeling a bit calmer but not any more content about her situation. But she had to get out of the shower at some point. She wrapped a towel around her torso, tucked it in at the top, then grabbed another one and rubbed her thick, tangled hair until it wasn't dripping.

A loud pounding on her door made her jump. Her heart kicked into a violent hammering in her chest as she peeked around the door of the bathroom.

Thankfully, she had used the deadbolt and the chain. She jumped as the pounding continued. Her heart jumped in her chest with each beat of the fist upon her door.

"I know you're in there. Open this door or I will call the police."

Levi. She closed her eyes, immediately recognizing the sound of Levi Tanner's voice.

His furious voice.

She swallowed hard and glanced at the bed where the memory card was hidden under the edge of the mattress. Inhaling a slow breath to attempt to steady her stomach, she crossed to the door, suddenly irritated at this cowboy who refused to leave her alone.

She yanked open the door. Levi stood there, his beautiful eyes hot with anger. She glared up at the tall, lean, dangerous man. He was a billionaire and she just needed a little bit of money. But she was doing a job; it wasn't as if she had stolen something…well, technically, she had stolen the photos of Cole and Tulip because she had been a wedding crasher, not invited to their special event.

Still, he needed to back off. "Would you stop banging on my door and go away? First, though, give me back my camera, please." *Why had she said please?*

He looked startled and only when his gaze slid down her body did she realize she was wearing just a towel. Instantly, her hand grasped the top edge to make sure it didn't come open.

His gaze shot back to meet hers. "I'm not going to give you back your camera. *You* are going to give me the memory card that went in that camera. That was a private wedding. It's not for wedding crashers to come in, snap photos, and then sell them for money. You people are sleazy and I'm sick of it. My brother and his bride just went through days and days of being hounded by you people, so the last thing they need is you putting pictures of them in the tabloids. And I guarantee you that's where your pictures are going to be in the morning. Aren't they?"

Her stomach dropped to the floor like a ten-ton rock. He had figured it out.

She tried not to look guilty, but at five-four, dark-headed, sweet-faced—at least, that's what she had always been told—and with big, sympathetic eyes, she probably looked guiltier than sin.

His eyes narrowed and she glared at him as guilt throbbed through her like an open wound. "The memory card belongs to me." *Don't tell him. Don't give it to him. You need it.*

"Oh, you'll give it to me. May I remind you that

the Tanners retain some of the best lawyers in the country. Lawyers who will be making your life very hard if you don't give me that memory card now. As a matter of fact, my top man is already preparing the documents that will be on their way here soon, Rita Snow."

Her mouth dropped open. "How do you know my name?"

"I'm from here—I have friends at the front desk. If that's your real name…it sounds fake."

"Maybe I need to get my own lawyer about the front desk. They aren't supposed to give out names."

"Oh, they didn't. They were in the back room while I looked on the computer screen."

She was so out of her league. "Yeah, right, probably after they opened up the account and then went in the back to give you time to look at the screen." She knew how that worked. She had seen it in the movies a lot. She shivered as a chill hit her. Even though it was a warm night, standing in front of her door with nothing but a towel on, a boatload of guilt wrapped around her like an ice pack. "I need you to leave. Please move your hand so I can close my door."

"Oh, no, you don't. I'm not going anywhere." And with that, he stepped inside and closed the door behind him.

She gasped and backed up, not really afraid of him but mad. Mad and weary. This was all going so wrong. "You have no right to be in this room."

He leaned against the doorframe and crossed his arms. "I'm not leaving until I get that memory card. And since I'm pretty sure I got here before you've had time to send it to your buyer, I figure if I lean against this door long enough or even camp out here, you won't have time to send them in. Those tabloids aren't getting those pictures. Cole and Tulip won't be on the cover of a gossip rag in the morning. And you won't be making money off their happy moment. Sorry," he finished snidely.

His words struck hard and true. "You're a jerk."

He laughed harshly as he thumbed his cowboy hat back on his head. "I've been called worse. What do you call yourself? A thief. Taking unauthorized pictures and selling them to the highest bidder. Doesn't that make your skin crawl? You look nicer than that. But I guess that's the deal—if you look all innocent like you do, then nobody suspects it."

His words hit home, making her feel even dirtier than she already did. She didn't flinch, though she was crumbling inside. They glared at each other and she refused to show how deep his words had cut. She saw all of her hopes die. If what he said was true, then she had already lost the money she would make from the pictures if she sent them in by eleven. The big payoff for the photographs would not be deposited into her bank account by tomorrow afternoon. This meant she wasn't going to be able to open her own business. She wasn't going to be able to make a home for her son.

Emotion clogged her throat. She might lose her son without the stability that she needed in order to keep her son supported.

Her insides caved and the sting of tears burned behind her eyes. Her knees went weak as emotions rolled over her like a bulldozer. Finally, unable to hold up, she sank to the edge of the bed, and dropped her elbows to her knees and then her forehead into her palms. Without the payoff, she very well could lose her son…he was her life.

Her heart hurt. Pain cut through her. She knew what she had been doing was wrong. Maybe there was no excuse, but she was desperate and now she was completely overwhelmed.

She fought hard to hold back a sob…but there was no holding it back.

* * *

Staring at Rita slumped on the edge of the bed— sobbing, if the shaking of her shoulders were any indication—Levi felt like a dog. Why, he wasn't sure. He was justified in his anger and determined to get the memory card and to keep Cole and Tulip off the front covers of the tabloids. They had gone through too much when they first met, and having their wedding splashed in the headlines just wasn't going to happen on his watch. All they wanted was to live a boring life, as Tulip called it, and he would do whatever he could to give her that. How had this woman gotten through the many layers of screening that had been done at the wedding in order to keep the paparats out, as he called them? She was one of them, he reminded himself as his anger faltered now. *Why was she crying?* This was unexpected.

Her dark wavy hair hung over her hands, exposing her shoulders. She had very nice shoulders, he couldn't help noticing. And legs. She had nice legs. The white hotel towel barely covered her body sitting there on the edge of the bed; they were very visible. He felt sleazy thinking about her legs when she was crying and wasn't happy about it.

She needed to get dressed. "It's obvious I'm going to be here for a while until you give me the memory card. Maybe you should put some clothes on."

Lifting her head, she wiped her eyes with trembling fingertips and then stood, carefully making sure the towel stayed in place. Her expression grim, she walked to the overnight bag on the dresser. She snatched a pair of jeans and a shirt from the bag and some pink underwear.

His pulse kicked in at the sight of the pink panties

and he felt uncomfortable. He didn't like the idea that he had busted in on her and she was in a vulnerable position wearing just that towel.

He ignored the fact that every time she looked at him, there was an undeniable flash of fire between them. Of course, it could just be that she was furious with him and he was furious with her. That kind of friction would cause a blaze.

Once he caused her to miss her deadline and had the memory card in his hands, he'd go back to his ranch and tending to his cattle, and she could go wherever it was that Rita Snow had come from.

He was still confused by her sudden crying after appearing so defiant. *Was it a ploy to get him to let her keep the memory card?* His lips flattened into a determined line as he hardened his resolve.

She strode across the room, into the bathroom, and closed the door behind her.

He glanced around the room, trying to figure out where she would have hidden that memory card. Probably in that bag. But the idea of going over and digging through her bag didn't sit well with him. But the way he looked at it, if he had to stand here all night so she couldn't load that memory card to her computer, then he'd do it.

Moments later, she walked out of the bathroom, looking fresh in the blue jeans, a yellow T-shirt and though he couldn't see them, he knew the hot-pink bra and panties were somewhere underneath the clothes.

He tried not to think about that.

"That's better. Now, could you give me the memory card and save us both some trouble? Then I'll go on my way and you can have the rest of the night here all by your lonesome."

She had calmed down while she was dressing, and she met him with cool eyes. "No. I'm going to call the police. You are in my room, and I didn't invite you in."

"No, I don't think you're going to call the police." He walked across the room and quickly unplugged the telephone, then took the phone and held it behind his back.

She walked over to the bag and pulled out her cell phone. And immediately pushed the keypad.

"Fine. Call 911. And when they get here, they'll probably haul both of us to jail. Fine by me since that'll mean you won't be emailing photos to anyone. Either way, I can assure you I'm going to get those photos off that memory card."

At least he hoped his claim about the photos would get her hauled in with him. His phone buzzed and he glanced at the incoming text from his lawyer that he had been delayed.

Of course. Now what?

Reason with her?

"Come on, be a human. What if you were getting married and some sleazy paparazzi person took personal pictures of you enjoying moments of pure happiness and sold them to the world to ogle at? A moment that you wanted to be private for just your friends and family, not to be sold to the highest bidder and be splashed across all the tabloids with who knows what headlines. Would you like that? You look like a nice person." She really did and that was what was so startling about all of this. She did not look slimy. She looked lovely.

She looked vulnerable again. Her gaze shifted downward.

He pushed forward in earnest. "I can't imagine that you do this for a living."

Guilt flickered in her beautiful eyes. She rubbed her forehead, took a deep breath and then she stuck her phone into her back pocket. "Fine, you win," she said, defeat in her voice as she crossed the room to the bed. She reached between the mattress and the box spring and pulled out the memory card.

He stepped forward and she laid it in his palm. His skin burned where she touched him and as she looked at him, there was no fire in her eyes, just defeat. And sadness.

He closed his fingers over the memory card. "Thank you." Unable to leave it at that and confused by the guilt that slammed into him the moment she'd given in, he had to ask, "Why would you do this? Surely there's some other job you can do. Instead of invading people's privacy."

She sank down on the edge of the bed. She had gone pale. "I'm not normally a person who does this.

I'm not a *paparazzi*." She said the word with as much venom as he felt for it. "I just need the money really bad. For me and my son." She looked away. "Anyway, it doesn't matter. I'm not going to give you my sob story. Just take the memory card and go. It was wrong of me. Go and I'll leave town in the morning."

He stared at her. He'd gotten what he wanted; he should be happy. But something in his gut would not let him leave. He crouched down in front of her and looked up into her downturned eyes. "Thank you for these files. How can I help you? I mean, honestly, you don't know how much this means to me that you gave me these photos. I'll be glad to help you. Just tell me what you need."

Boy, she could con him right now, but something told him this part of tonight was not a con. He was a pretty good poker player; he had a good poker face and he could read people normally and he did not feel as though she were playing him. Not anymore.

"I'm not going to take charity from you, Mr. Tanner. So even though you classify what I was doing as sleazy, it was a job. I was getting paid for it. And I wasn't taking charity."

"I don't see anything wrong with somebody taking a helping hand when they need it. Especially from someone who has the means to help them and is very willing to do so. Do you need a job? I can give you a job, if that's what you need. If that will help you out, believe me, we've got all kinds of jobs on our ranch and in our various businesses. Seriously, I can help you out. And then you won't be taking charity."

He was talking out of the top of his head. He had never ever thought he'd be chasing a wedding crasher down and then be trying to convince her to take a job from him. It had really been a strange evening. But she was desperate for some reason and he was so relieved that this wasn't a gig she normally did that he wanted to do whatever he could to help her.

CHAPTER THREE

Rita stared at the unbelievably handsome cowboy crouched down in front of her with the sincerest expression on his face. She had never taken charity. Her pride settled over her. She thought about Toby and the life she wanted to give him that would be so much better than what she had been raised with. She was tempted. But she couldn't do it. "You don't want to hire me."

His expression turned stubborn. "Now hold on, I told you I wanted to hire you and now you're calling me a liar?"

"Well, no, I'm not. I just tried to sell pictures of your brother, for crying out loud. I'm a terrible person."

He closed one eye and squinted at her through the other. "I'm thinking you're not. I'm thinking…" He opened both eyes. "I think you're desperate. There's this part of me, the stubborn part, that wants to know why a woman would do something as desperate as trying to turn into a sleazeball and sell pictures of my brother and his bride. It has to be something real important, I'm thinking."

The man was aggravating; it was as if he could read her mind. She still felt slimy, but she had been desperate. "Look, you might be right but that still doesn't mean you need to give me a job. What if I'm not who you think I am?"

He stood up and paced across the room, giving her a great view of his strong, lean body in his now wet and crumpled clothes that had been perfectly starched jeans and crisp white shirt at the wedding. Earlier, he had had on a jacket but somewhere along the way he had taken it off. He'd looked so amazing at the wedding but even now, he was every bit the gorgeous cowboy who had done everything he could to protect his family's privacy. Including destroying her dreams.

But she had been in the wrong. Levi was one of the good guys—a billionaire but a good guy—because right now he was looking past all she had done and insisting on giving her a job.

The tabloids had loved stories about these brothers—the reluctant billionaires was what they were sometimes called. Everybody knew their story. In these parts, when oil hit, sometimes it was big. She knew in the Hill Country there was a lot of money hidden in these ranches, behind their secluded iron fences. And this guy, Levi Tanner, was one of the wealthiest. Her plan had just been to sneak in, get the photos and get out, get her money and open up her photography business; she and Toby would be in good shape after a little while, after she got up and running. Now she had messed it all up.

He turned toward her, making her realize she was lost in thought.

He put a hand on his hip, and she noticed the college ring. It was easy to see the A&M emblem on it. She had read that he and most of his brothers had gone to Texas A&M. The others had gone to other Texas colleges and were proud to be Texans. She had read a lot about them. She knew that they were ranchers; they loved their land and they loved their family. They pretty much wanted to be left alone and almost didn't know what to do with all that money that they had. And now he was offering to give her a job. He could afford it. Could she let herself accept the offer? She couldn't feel any lower than she did right now after trying to take advantage of him.

When she didn't say anything, he did. "Rita, level with me. Tell me why you took the pictures. I think you owe me that, and then let me go from there."

She rubbed her hands on her thighs. "You're right. I do owe you at least an explanation. I'm a photographer. I take photos of families and weddings normally. I'm good at what I do. But I lost my job recently because I wouldn't sleep with my boss. And then he spread the word that I tried to steal his clients and then tried to seduce him. I got another job and soon learned my new boss believed the sleeping around part. I quit." The thought of it all made her skin crawl. "It was their word against mine, and my bosses all had really good reputations."

He scowled and her heart fluttered, looking at him.

What if she did accept his offer and he turned out to be just as rotten as her last two bosses?

She shuddered at this thought. She would be so disappointed if he turned out to be a bad guy. Looks were deceiving—she had learned that from her last boss, who looked like a choirboy. He was so sweet-looking and easygoing, but it had all been a lie, she found out.

"Anyway, I left the Panhandle and came down here thinking I would open my own photography business, and then I could take care of my little boy. My mother has him right now and my mother-in-law is trying to take him from me. I made this big mistake coming here and thinking if I took these pictures and took the paycheck then I'd be set. All I'd have to do is rent my building and open my doors. And I'd start a business of my own and no one could think about taking my son from me."

He had been quiet, watching her. "So are the rumors true? Is that why she's trying to take your son?"

"No." Disappointment rolled over her like a wave

of ice water. He had a right to ask; she had confessed it to him. "You probably think the worst of me because I have been acting not in good faith but no, I did not try to steal their clients or seduce them. I'm a good mother. I'm just trying to get a new start. And my mother-in-law is just trying to fill the hole in her heart left by the death of her son and then her husband, who died not too long ago."

"Okay, so it sounds like you need a break. Sounds like you need an investor. Not just a job."

She stood. "No. No—you offered me a job, now you're saying an investor. No, that's just too much. I can't do that."

"Tell you what. If you promise me you'll stay here and get a good night's sleep and that you'll be here in the morning, then I'll come back and we'll talk about this over breakfast, a late breakfast. It is late and my brother wore me out before the wedding, getting things ready. So, let's both start over. We'll discuss this then, when we're both rested. I'll be back in the morning. But you have to promise me that you'll be here."

She stared at him. She didn't make promises idly.

But if she told him no, he probably wouldn't leave. "Okay, I promise. Maybe after you get some sleep you'll think sensibly."

He moved to the door and she walked with him. She could smell his cologne. She felt a little dizzy, the man smelled so good.

Levi turned at the door and looked down at her. "I'm not going to change my mind, so don't worry about that, Rita Snow. Sleep well and I'll be back around ten o'clock. How does that sound?"

She nodded, weary. "It sounds perfect."

He smiled at her and her heart turned over. She told it to straighten up and quit doing that. This was not somebody she could get a crush on or any of that business. This was all strictly business. *If* she did business with him. That was still up in the air.

"Talk to you tomorrow." Then he opened the door and he was gone.

She stared at the door and walked over and sank back down on the bed. This had been one of the worst days of her life. One of the weirdest days of her life. But she knew that if she gave in to his offer of help, it could very well be one of the best days of her life.

* * *

"You did what?" His brother Jake stared at him with a look of complete confusion on his face.

Levi felt a little confused himself. After having left Rita at the hotel room with the camera disk in his hand, he had wondered whether he had lost his mind. But he hadn't let himself dwell on it too hard; instead, he had driven home, taken a shower, climbed in bed, and tried to relax. It had been a long week, getting ready for Cole and Tulip's wedding. Plus, his mom and dad had come to town; they hadn't been in town for six months with all the traveling they had been doing after their move to their new beachside home in Florida.

He and his brothers might struggle adjusting to all this money they had come into but his parents, once they had gotten used to the idea, had thrown themselves into traveling and seeing the world. They were good people, salt of the earth, and they deserved the life of luxury that they had decided to enjoy. His mother had said they were only doing it for now because they didn't have any grandkids but when they got grandkids, they'd come home. They'd still do some traveling, but they'd be spending more time around the boys, the boys being him and his four brothers.

His mom still called them "the boys" even though they were all in their thirties or near thirties. He smiled, thinking about his mom. She had been so happy last night. So had Tulip's mom. And all those ladies who had flocked around Tulip's mama's table— her friends and clients from her hair salon who had all been invited. They'd been thrilled to see their Tulip, as they called her, get married. It had been a happy time and he had enjoyed it very much. Except for not being able to relax because he was worried about photographers sneaking in. He'd been tense, worrying, and then when he'd spied Rita taking shots she shouldn't have been taking, he freaked out a little bit. Probably overreacted. But then again, he had gotten the photo disk, and if there were any photos that had gotten out, it wouldn't be from her disk. He felt good about that. They deserved some private time. But as his eyes closed, the pretty face of Rita Snow with her big, beautiful, sad eyes filled his mind as he drifted off to sleep.

Now, staring at his brother, who had met him at

the barn this morning, he gave a tepid smile. "You heard me right. I traced the gal who took the photos to the hotel room after the limo had dropped her off, and I confronted her last night. Couldn't let her get away with it. She had snuck that disk out of her camera that I had confiscated at the scene of the crime, and I was determined to get it back. And she did give it to me. And she confessed that she was down on her luck and that's why she had been taking the pictures. She seemed like a really nice person."

Jake scowled. "Levi, you are about the most leery person in this family. You barely even walk around without your hat pulled down over your face so nobody can recognize you these days. You are so wary of having your picture taken and now that you ran this woman down and she had conned you, you're saying she's a nice person? And you think she's going to still be at that hotel room when you get back this morning?"

"I know it sounds stupid on my part, but she promised me she would stay and that we would discuss this over breakfast."

"Breakfast? And that you would discuss you giving her a job?"

"Yeah. I mean, I can afford it. We've got plenty of things on the ranch to plug people in. Just trying to figure out what kind of job to give her but she doesn't want to take it. I offered just to set her up in her own photography business, set her up in a little store. We've got some property down on the main strip in Fredericksburg. It was a good investment, I think, but we haven't done anything with it, so why not give her a storefront?"

"Brother, you have lost your mind. Nobody else is going to believe you're saying this either."

He looked out over the paddock where the horses were frisky this morning, running around with their tails held high. They had more energy than he had this morning. He had slept but not very long because, by the time he'd got to bed, it was almost two a.m. And now it was eight.

"Look, maybe I have, but I just have a feeling that she's not lying. I can't help it."

"And I bet she's really pretty, too, isn't she? I

didn't get a good look at her last night—I was busy dancing."

So, there it was. "Yeah, she's real pretty. But she's had a hard time and that doesn't mean anything. If I give her a job, it's hands off. She's been mistreated by bosses, so it's not that. If I was interested in her, I wouldn't be giving her a job. I'd be asking her out on a date. So, there solves your problem. Giving her a job— if she'll take it—will help her out so she can make a good life for her and her little boy. What's wrong with that?"

"Nothing," his brother drawled, eyeing him with a hitched brow that said he was being sarcastic.

Levi rubbed his jaw. "Yeah, I know you're right. It is all kind of crazy but I'm a man of my word. I offered her a job, and if she's there this morning like she promised, then I'm going to give her a job. Then I'm going to offer her a storefront when she finishes the job. If she'll take it. Now I need to figure out a job to give her."

Jake took his hat off and slapped it on his thigh as he studied the horses.

Levi wasn't sure whether he was thinking about a job or trying to figure out how to dissuade him from making the offer. He waited and let his mind roll over different places he could hire Rita for on the ranch.

Jake looked at him. "How about this—we got that big sale coming up and we need to hire a photographer to take pictures of all our bulls and heifers that we're going to put in it. She's a photographer—why not offer her that job? It will take a couple weeks at least to get all those photos taken. Of course, we've got a month, so she can go slow and you can pay her well. You know it's never cheap to hire a photographer so you could just pad the payment a little and then maybe she'd have some money to rent one of those buildings in Fredericksburg. And, we're buying that place in Montana—we need photos of that place, too. Why don't you take her down in the jet, drive her around and have her take some shots for us? We're going to need it documented."

That was a good idea. Well, actually both of them were a good ideas. He grinned at his brother. "Wow, why didn't I think of any of that? Those are excellent ideas. I can present both of them when I see her this morning."

Jake grinned at him. "Yeah, and then when she's not working for you in a month, then you can ask her out because you know you want to. You wouldn't be doing this if you weren't interested."

That kind of made him feel bad. "You're saying I wouldn't do a good deed if it didn't involve her being attractive? That's not true."

Jake put his hat back on. "I'm not saying that completely. But in this situation, since it involves photographers and I know just how bad you dislike paparazzi, I think it's got your mind just a little bit twisted up and not thinking straight."

Feeling irritated, Levi glared at his brother. "I'm not mixed up. Yeah, I hate them. I'll never get over the way they hounded us and lied about us when we first struck oil. They scrutinized our every move. I made mistakes and they dragged me through horse crap because of it. We were as famous as a stinkin' boy band. I was so tired of them."

Jake looked disgusted. "I know. It was ridiculous.

And I'm no fonder of them than you are. I just wanted to keep being ranchers and working the ranch, like we've always done. But nope, the paparats trailed us like dogs, snapping photos everywhere we went."

"And looking for anything to post about us to sell to a tabloid." Levi's blood pressure rose just talking about it. And it hadn't just been in the Hill Country; some of them had been nationwide. Yeah, it had been a hard time in their lives, adjusting to the money *and* the publicity.

He had grown up under the limelight in the last few years. For the last two years, he'd tried his hardest to blend in with the shadows when he was out. He had elaborate ways to get off his ranch when the paparats were in town, and he drove an old beat-up truck no one would ever believe belonged to a billionaire. For the most part, he'd stayed off their radar for the last couple of years.

And now Rita had shown up. He'd been angry and maybe he should still be angry, but something about her just wouldn't let him be. Maybe it was that he was attracted to her like nothing he'd ever known before.

Whatever it was, he just had to give her a shot. She'd given the files back to him and he would not let that go. He would help her. And that was that.

Rita's sad eyes filled his thoughts and how his blood just kind of heated up when she looked at him. He had seen that flame flicker in her eyes, too, and he could not help but wonder what would happen when they were past all this. What if they had met under normal circumstances?

The truth was, he was getting tired of eating alone and living out on the ranch by himself. And watching Cole and Tulip these last few months be so happy had gotten him to thinking long and hard about finding someone special.

The thing about finding someone special was you couldn't do it if you didn't date. You couldn't do it if you didn't pursue when you felt an interest in someone. And there was no denying how much interest he had in Rita Snow.

CHAPTER FOUR

Rita hadn't slept much and woke early, as the sun filtered between the cheap curtains that didn't fit well at the top. She lay there feeling as if she'd been run over by an eighteen-wheeler. Depression flattened her on the bed and held her down like a heavy weight sat on her chest and she just couldn't make herself get up.

What had she been thinking last night?

She groaned and closed her eyes as shame rolled over her at all the bad choices she'd made. She couldn't make any more bad choices. As desperate as she'd been when she'd made the choice to crash the Tanner wedding, take photos, and sell them for a profit to the tabloids, it was a bad idea and inexcusable. Yes, she had been desperate to find a way to support her son so that her mother-in-law wouldn't find a way to take him from her. But using someone wasn't the way to do it.

Levi Tanner filled her mind—and his remarkable offer.

As mad as he'd been, his generous and unlikely offer to give her a job had touched her deeply. And made her feel all the worse for what she'd tried to do. She felt small and teary-eyed, thinking about his amazing offer. But would accepting it be another bad choice? He seemed so sincere—could she take a chance on him?

She forced herself out of bed and after a shower, she dressed, zipped up her small duffel bag full of her things, and headed outside to wait on him. Standing in the parking lot with the duffel at her feet and her purse hanging from her shoulder, she realized she had no car. *How could she have forgotten she didn't have a car?* She had been so upset last night that she'd completely forgotten that the last time she'd seen her car, it was half submerged in the pond at the wedding venue. She couldn't have left this morning if she'd wanted to.

She still might have time to call a taxi—if this tiny town had a taxi. She'd bet they didn't. *Too late, anyway*, she thought as Levi, driving an old beat-up pickup, pulled into the parking lot. She stared at his truck in disbelief. It was a rusty mess.

The truck lurched to a halt. He jumped from the driver's seat and jogged around the front of his truck and over to her. He looked happy, energetic, and so very handsome as he beamed a grin at her that took her breath away. Her heart seized up and her stomach did too. She thought maybe her ulcer had been acting up. She'd been taking medicine for it, so hopefully this wasn't it ramping back up. She was a basket case, for a twenty-five-year-old.

"Hey, up there. You ready for some breakfast?" He sounded as if she were some old friend he was taking to breakfast. Not the woman who had tried to sell his brother's wedding photos to a sleazy magazine.

"Sure, coffee sounds fabulous. And some eggs."

He grinned at her. "Well, I'm having pancakes. You did good picking this motel to stay in. Dixie's here in Stonewall has the best pancakes in the world."

She'd picked this small town and its rundown motel because it had the cheapest room price and looked cleaner than the other old motels she'd stopped and asked about. "I can do a pancake. That sounds great."

"Trust me, it is." He reached for her bag.

And his cologne wafted over her.

Wow. Bold and fresh, it reminded her of leather and fresh rain. He smelled amazing. She took a step back because it was that or launch herself at him. That wouldn't be good.

He paused as he put the shoulder strap on his shoulder. "You're not afraid of me, are you?"

"Oh no, no. Not at all." She blushed and her skin heated. "Sorry. I'm just nervous." That wasn't a lie. She wasn't comfortable with people breaking her personal space.

"Look, no need to be with me. Now let's go get some breakfast. Dixie's is a little café on the corner— we can eat breakfast there and talk. I have a plan that I think you might be interested in."

The man sounded all too happy this morning. It

was just weird. *Did having billions of dollars at your disposal make you a happy person like that? Or was he just losing it? Or was he just a nice guy trying to help her out?* She felt so cynical, thinking the worst about everybody. That question hit a little too close for comfort. When had she lost so much faith in everybody around her? It was just the wrong way to go through life, and it certainly wasn't the way she wanted to raise Toby. She wanted Toby to grow up knowing that there was good in this world. Yes, there were bad people and people with differing views but it was still a good place.

She smiled at Levi. "That sounds great. And, honestly, I'm surprised that you really turned back up here this morning. But since I realized I didn't even have a car this morning and I was kind of stuck, I'm grateful that you showed up. And if your idea sounds at all promising, then I'm willing to listen."

His smile was dazzling, and she told her insides, where the butterflies were doing flip-flops: *Calm down and stop being silly. He's not interested in you like that. He's just being nice. He's just a super nice man.*

He led the way to the truck and opened the door for her. "After you."

A gentleman, too.

"Thank you." She sucked in another breath of his great cologne as she stepped past him and slid into the seat. He closed the door. It creaked with age as he rammed it shut. *Why did this billionaire drive this heap of a truck?*

He set her bag in the truck's bed then jogged back around to his side. His door creaked too as he opened it. She noticed the seat was so old it had an indentation where his butt went, where the springs had been worn down. And there was duct tape holding the aged leather look-a-like material together where he sat down.

"Are you into fixing up old vehicles?" she asked.

He slid a hand onto the steering wheel and pulled the gearshift into drive as he looked at her. "No. Why do you ask?"

Okay, that was weird. "Well, you're driving this…" How did she say *this dump*?

He grinned before she could answer. "You think my truck is a wreck?"

Her mouth went dry. "A little."

He laughed. "You are insulting my truck. I am hurt. Stunned."

"Sorry, but it is, kind of. It squeaks and your seat looks uncomfortable. You're sitting in a hole over there with tape to hold it together."

His eyes danced. "Yep, this was my granddaddy's ranch truck. It's a good one. And when I pull this wide-brimmed hat down over my eyes, I can drive right through the middle of a bunch of nosey photographers and they don't give me a second glance. Not even a first glance."

She stared at him, her mouth dropping open, and then she busted out laughing.

* * *

He pulled up to the diner and parked in the slanted parking space. "It doesn't look like much, but I promise you once you taste her pancakes, you'll never be satisfied with anything but Dixie's pancakes. She's known far and wide for how good they are. Not sure what her secret ingredient is but it's magical."

She laughed and he liked the sound of it.

"I can't wait. And I was going to be good and have some protein, but now my mouth is watering for carbs."

He held up his hands and shrugged. "You can eat protein all you want but some mornings are just pancake mornings. This is one of those mornings. Come on. Here, I'll get the door for you."

"I can get my own door." She pushed on her door but it wouldn't open.

He knew it wouldn't. It always got stuck. "You're denying me the privilege of opening your door for you and making my mama proud."

She hesitated and stopped trying to open the door. "Okay. I'll wait."

He hopped out of the truck, slammed his door, and jogged around to her side, then yanked the door for her. She smiled at him as she slid out of the truck.

There were a lot of trucks outside as this was a favorite breakfast spot for local cowboys and those from surrounding counties. When they entered the diner, it was pretty full since it was still mid-breakfast morning time.

Dixie, a plump little lady, bristled by, grinning. She had hair stacked up high on top of her head and carried two plates of pancakes stacked almost as high as her hair. "Good morning, Levi. You, too, young lady. Y'all have a seat wherever you want. Sheri will be over to take your order. That little seat over there by the window is a nice one."

Levi grinned at Dixie. "Thanks, Dixie. This is Rita, and we've come for pancakes."

Dixie laughed. "I should have known. Nice to meet you, Rita. Levi's one of my best customers. Everybody's about to wear me out with these pancakes."

They went to the table next to the window. It was a table for two and it wasn't very big. Therefore, when they sat down across from each other, they were fairly close. He didn't mind at all.

"Those do look delicious."

"I told you, they're fantastic. So buttery. And I think there's vanilla in there and maybe some almond. There's something in there—they almost taste like a cake."

Soon they'd made their order, and both sat drinking their coffee while they waited.

"You said you have a little boy. How old is he?"

"Four. His name is Toby, and he's an awesome little kid. Even if he is mine."

He liked the way her eyes sparkled when she talked about little Toby. "Does he like being outdoors?"

"He loves it. He'd rather be outside than inside, which isn't always easy to do. He's a busy boy and very curious. I adore him and love him to the moon and back."

"He's a very lucky kid."

She smiled at him. "Thank you."

The pancakes showed up about that time. Stacked high, the buttery, golden pancakes were so fluffy they looked as if they might float. There were five plate-sized pancakes on each of their plates. Her eyes widened because it was obvious that she hadn't fully absorbed what a stack of pancakes from Dixie's looked like up close.

He chuckled. "A bit overwhelming up close, aren't they?"

She laughed. "Just a little." She looked from him to the smiling waitress. "You should have warned me," she said as the scent of warm pancakes, vanilla, and a touch of almond filled the air. "My mouth is watering just smelling these." She leaned forward, closed her eyes, and breathed in the scents. "Heavenly."

The waitress laughed. "It's too fun watching people's first reactions. Just wait till you try them. You'll surprise yourself with how much of that stack you eat. They are addictive and ain't none better in the state—or the world, I'd venture to say. It's her special ingredient that she refuses to give up."

"Okay, and on that note, I'm digging in. I am starving, so I'll make sure I balance out the carbohydrate overload with the strips of bacon included. Thanks."

"Sure thing. Enjoy." The waitress hurried off to take a check to another table.

Rita poured syrup on top of the stack and then sliced into them. She took a bite and a smile came to her mouth as she chewed, and her eyes closed as she finished the first bite. "Amazing. Amazing. Amazing," she managed as she barely swallowed and then dug in for a second bite.

He smiled. "Yup. Right on all counts." He dug in and they ate for a few minutes until they began to fill the dent in their hunger. He knew they'd eat more, but both of them slowed on the pace of chugging them down. "Amazing." He chuckled, copying her statement. "We are in agreement about that." He picked up his coffee and took a sip.

The waitress saw him and stopped by with a pot to top off their cups. She grinned. "You're doing Dixie proud—you're halfway to finished."

"And not stopping yet." Rita took a sip of coffee. "Thanks. I love them."

The waitress gave a thumbs-up and headed off to refresh others' coffee.

He took a breath. "So, here's the deal, now that we're letting the first half settle before we finish these off. I'm hoping you've kind of gotten to get to know me a little bit better and figured out that I'm not the terrible guy I probably made you think I was last night. And I don't think you are the person I thought you were, and I am very thankful for that. I'd like it if we could just forget the whole incident. We started out on the wrong foot and I'd like us to start fresh."

She held her cup with both hands cupped around it and looked at him over the brim. "I agree." She lowered the cup and smiled at him.

He really did like that smile. Jake had not been off on his figuring out that Levi was attracted to this pretty woman. Because it was true. She was doing all this crazy stuff because she wanted to make life better for her little boy. Wasn't as if she were doing something illegal. Just irritating.

"Okay, so, this morning, I talked with my brother Jake. He's my youngest brother and he's a good fella. He came up with a great idea. We've got a big cattle sale coming up. But the not so fun part is somebody's got to take the pictures of all the cattle. Now, if you're a photographer and you enjoy that sort of thing, I guess it would be fun. Me having to find somebody willing to come take all those photographs isn't fun. So, we were thinking maybe we would hire you on for a month, and you can take all the pictures of our cattle that need to be taken.

"Then there's this other issue that we have. We bought a new ranch just recently. The final sale went through and we have some plans for that ranch, and we need professional photographs of the different portions of land—the parts that would stand out and make the land special. Valuable to anybody for gorgeous land and not just cattle land. Anyway, it's in Montana, and we need somebody to go out there and take those pictures. Now the plan is I'll fly out there with you and give you the tour while you take the shots. I need to check the land out, too, since I haven't actually been out there. Jake went initially and the rest of us bought it off his recommendations. I'm eager to see it. It's supposed to be gorgeous, and I do have a love affair with pretty ranch land."

She set her cup down and he wasn't sure what she was thinking. She looked stunned, so he continued, "It's easily a month's worth of work. No charity involved, and a cabin and meals provided for you and Toby. I'll pay you well and will do some upfront if you need it, and along the way. If we need to keep you on for longer, we'd like to do that too, if you have the time. And how would you feel about a business in Fredericksburg? You know, that's kind of the mecca of Hill Country and a lot of weddings go on there. We own some very prime real estate on the main street, and we'd make you a good deal on rent."

"Why would you do that?" Her voice was barely audible.

"Because you're nice and we really want to rent the place out to somebody who might want to stay long-term. There's a particularly good spot that's got an apartment above it and that might be the perfect situation for you and Toby. At the end of the month, you could lease that from us at a low price. You'll have enough money saved up because you can live on the ranch while all this stuff is going on and bring your little boy out to live with you. The cabins are very nice. And food is provided at the chow hall morning, noon, and dinner if you want it. Or there is a kitchen in the cabin if you prefer to cook. We have guests who stay in the cabins from time to time, but we have plenty and no guests right now."

He smiled, hoping she'd take the job. Hoping

she'd be around long enough for him to get to know her better.

Rita looked shocked. "It's a very generous offer and exactly what I need, but really, are you serious?"

"I'm serious as a heart attack. We really do need these jobs done. And I need to see the Montana ranch, so it's as if you were meant to be here. Take the job." He wanted to put his hand on hers and urge her to take the job, but he kept his hands firmly on his side of the table.

Her face was one of complete confusion. He could see her mind working behind those beautiful eyes of hers as she probably thought about all the things he had said and most likely weighed all the different elements of her own life. He waited patiently, letting her think all she wanted. He took another sip of his coffee. He really hoped she said yes.

Was it wrong to hire her because he wanted to help her but also to get to know her better? The thought of spending a whole week in Montana with her sounded especially nice. He could be a gentleman and wanted her to learn that about him. He wasn't always the idiot she'd met last night. He wanted a chance to prove that to her. From what she'd said last night, she hadn't been treated right by her last couple of bosses and he wanted to change that for her. He could be a real good guy and then, when she wasn't working for him any longer, maybe she'd go out with him.

He liked the plan; he liked it a lot.

And one of the things he liked the most about it was they'd be away from all the craziness and nobody would even know that they were hanging out together. They'd use a private jet service to get them out to Montana and back, and the rest of the time they'd be on his ranch behind iron gates. He was in his old truck, and had come out of the ranch on one of his hidden exits, and they were eating at an off-the-beaten-track diner, ensuring that if there were any leftover vultures hanging around who'd waited at the entrance to the wedding venue then they wouldn't latch onto him.

"I'll take the job."

He grinned—couldn't help it. His smile spread across his face and probably wrapped around his ears, it was so big. "Well, that makes me very happy, as you can tell by my smile."

She laughed and rubbed her temple, looking at him with eyes now that said she was still not believing it was really happening. Boy, he liked being able to shock somebody like that, especially after having made them think he was a terrible person the night before.

"Well then, I think we have ourselves a deal. I haven't even told you what the salary is but I promise you that you're going to like the pay."

"As long as it's fair then I'm good. And something tells me that you're a very fair man."

"And I like the sound of that, because I do try. Again, my mom would have my hide if I was anything but honest and fair." And that was the truth.

CHAPTER FIVE

"Yes, Mom. It's an amazing deal. That's what I told him. I'm going to take pictures of cattle and then go out to his ranch in Montana with him. So, this will be helpful with Laura wanting to take Toby away from me."

"I hope you're right. That woman scares me. After what her son did to you, and now she thinks she can just keep Toby…I'm so scared."

Her heart ached, listening to her mother. Glinda , who Toby affectionally called Grammy, did not need the stress of worrying about this. "Don't be worried, Mom. I'm going to get this figured out. She is still mourning the loss of her son and husband and thinks my Toby is the answer. And in a way he is. Just not full-time. I have no problem with him being loved by all of his grandparents, but he belongs with me. And I believe God has given me a way to keep him. Levi has been amazing. So don't worry. Everything is going to be all right."

She had to be right. Had to be. If Laura could somehow prove Rita was incompetent and could not care for her Toby, Rita feared Laura could have a case. And she knew all too well that life was not always on her side.

"Levi has so far proved he's a good guy. So, I have to trust that he is. I have to trust that everything is going to be okay and that Toby will not be stolen away from me."

She stopped swinging in the porch swing and stood. She looked around the ranch that spread out before her. It was an amazing stone house up the hill from the cabins; the barns and stables were traditional red metal with silver-toned metal roofs. What he'd pointed out as the bunkhouse and the chow hall matched the barns. And then there were the round pens and the roping pens and the beautiful pastures that spread out around it all. And here, from the porch of this amazing cottage—or cabin, as he called it—the view was outstanding.

It was an unbelievably beautiful place. She couldn't believe she was here. He'd called the rental car company and settled up with them since he'd said she ran in the water because of him. She'd told him she could take care of it but he'd insisted and told her he had plenty of ranch trucks that she could use while she was here and didn't need to bring her own car in from Amarillo or rent another car. He'd been so generous and here she was. Still not believing her good luck being on this beautiful ranch. Levi had told her that this was the ranch he managed. The family owned several ranches; down the way was the ranch his brother Cole ran that had been the original ranch, and his brother Jake ran another ranch down the road a ways. And now they had bought the ranch in Montana and expanding. It was clear they had the money to do whatever they wanted but he'd said it was because they loved ranching; it was in their blood.

She believed him. The funny thing was, he mentioned the money very little.

She knew from Googling him that ranching was a tradition in their family and that the ranch that they had struck oil on had been in their family for decades. Obviously, the oil that had sat beneath that ground had been unattainable until the extracting technology had developed that could get to it. And when it had struck, it had struck in a monstrous way, completely taking the family by surprise. She liked that Levi didn't like to talk about it because it made him seem more like a regular cowboy, just working a ranch and trying to make a living.

She realized her mom was still talking and she pulled back her attention. "Yes, Mom, so I'll come out in a couple of days—maybe three, I'll let you know. I'll get Toby and bring him back here. The more time he's with me, the better at this point. I just need to see what my job will be like and my hours, then I'll be there. Levi says Toby's welcome to come. He even suggested it. He's going to love it here. He'll be able to go with me while I'm taking pictures." She laughed. "I need to make sure Levi understands how busy a four-year-old can be."

Her mother laughed. "That would be good for him to know. I love keeping him, my energy level just doesn't hold out with all of his energy."

She knew what her mother said was the truth. Her Lupus caused havoc with her energy and her body hurting, especially her back, and made keeping Toby much more than a week almost impossible. The recovery time for her was getting longer and longer. Chronic illness was a terrible thing and really stressed her out because she wanted to do so much more than she could. "You've been a huge help, but I can't wait to see him. I miss him so bad."

She had only been away from him for three days and hoped to pick him up within the next two. She'd been afraid she was going to have to be away from him for long periods of time if she couldn't figure out a way to make a living. That would have made it hard on her mother and easier for Laura to claim she should have custody of him. Levi caused hope to bloom in her chest. She'd felt that way since their breakfast, and that hope was so much sweeter and fulfilling than even Dixie's amazing pancakes.

"Thank you so much for watching him, Mom. And if you need me, call, okay? I'm just so full of excitement right now, thinking about how at the end of this month I'll be able to open my own business on the strip in Fredericksburg. It's such a beautiful place. And after I get there, I'll bring you out and you'll be able to see. And who knows? You may decide you want to move in this direction."

Her mother made excuses and said she had all of her friends out there in Amarillo. It would be hard to get her mom to move but a grandson was a good incentive. And Rita held out hope she could change her mother's mind when the time came. If the time came.

Her heart clenched tight; she closed her eyes and said a prayer that everything would turn out all right. That her child would not be taken away from her.

This ranch was perfect. A lot of cowboys moved about; some were with horses in arenas, and some walked around, leading horses. It was obvious to see that though it was called a cattle ranch, Levi's ranch did a lot of stuff with horses. It was a busy place. But over here, where her little cabin sat, it was quiet. There were other cabins, but they were all spaced out a fairly decent width from each other, and it didn't look as though anybody else was living in the other cabins. Levi said they didn't have any special guests right now, so she had this area all to herself. She was a little relieved by that. She didn't want to be all the way over here with some strangers she really didn't know, living within a few feet of her.

The cabin was adorable. It was yellow with a porch and a swing, and there was even a back patio with a little table that overlooked a pasture that was down below the hillside. She had a great view in the back of the cabin, but she found that she was enjoying the view of all the business going on with the ranch right now. It was just her curiosity. Then again, there was the fact that from where she stood, she could see Levi moving around. He talked to all the cowboys, directing them in what he wanted to do, and she could see that he was busy and that he was in control. She figured that Levi Tanner might seem like a happy-go-lucky young cowboy, when he wasn't fiercely fighting off people taking photos of his family, but that guy was serious about his ranching.

He loved it. And he knew what he was doing. He might have all that money but she had a feeling that even without that money his ranch would be a success.

She went inside, looked around the adorable little cabin and felt hope rising up again. The Texas-themed rooms were well done. Even the cattle skull hanging on the wall was pretty, the way it was decorated with dried flowers. There was a cattle skin rug on the floor, which again, all Texans were used to seeing that. The furniture was beautiful, made of what looked like mesquite wood and clear-coated to a shine that glistened. Everything was perfect.

Small but perfect for her and Toby.

She sat down at the dining table, cupped her hands together, and said a prayer of thanksgiving. And she prayed that she wasn't being fooled. Even though she didn't think she was, there would probably always be a leery feeling inside her. After the last couple of jobs she had and then her husband's lies…she might never get over the feelings of distrust.

But she wanted so badly for Levi to be who he said he was. And for this job to be real.

* * *

Levi had had to spend a little bit of time with ranch business after showing Rita her cabin. She had loved it and he was glad. They had gone through a good bit of expense to make the cabins nice here and at the other two ranches. Before they had made all that money, when the ground had pretty much exploded like a cash machine at a casino giving out the winning payout, they'd made some improvements on the ranch because they all loved ranching. Then they bought more ranches in the area and continued to do so. He, for one, could give away all that money and just have his little piece of heaven right here on this ranch.

He'd used the money to update everything and had enjoyed spending money on the cabins to make them nice for guests with some good comforts of Texas. Heck, even the new bunkhouse he'd built for his guys farther into the ranch interior was built of Austin stone and had all the luxuries any cowboy could want. It even had a pool table and indoor or outdoor shower, depending on what the cowboys wanted, and plenty of full-size bunks rather than little twin-sized mattresses. He figured the better they slept at night, the better they worked. He wanted the guys who worked for him to want to work for him. He knew what sleeping on an uncomfortable mattress felt like because he'd spent some time in high school summers helping out on other ranches when needed.

His dad always said working for someone else would give them a different perspective for when it came their time to hire ranch help. It would help them understand what it took to be fair to both the men they hired and themselves. Dad had been right in his thoughts. He'd led by example, but it had been a good lesson to see that not everyone treated their hired help like their dad did. Levi tried to live up to the standard of his dad.

Finally, after taking care of the business he needed to get done and after giving Rita time to settle in, he jumped in his ATV and headed toward the cabin to pick her up. Of all the things the money had enabled him to do here on the ranch and the charities they donated to, he had to admit that having the ability to help Rita out had felt the best of all.

She stood up from where she had been crouched down, taking a picture with her camera of one of the rosebushes that they had transplanted from the original ranch here. Their mother loved roses and they planned to make sure they always had plenty of them on the properties.

"I see you've found my mother's roses. She loves them. Yellow roses especially."

"They're beautiful."

"Thanks. Mom planted a whole bunch of them up at the original ranch that Cole runs, so we brought some here. Tulip did a great job landscaping over there, and I'm hoping she'll do some here too. That's her specialty. I'll have to take you by—it's beautiful. I can't let Cole out-do me. Are you taking pictures of the flowers?"

She beamed at him and there was a lightness to her smile, as if she had relaxed some. Maybe she was feeling less stress than she'd been feeling; if that were so, then that made his day.

"Well, I am, but mostly I'm taking a picture of the bee that's getting pollen off the roses. I love bees and butterflies and hummingbirds and all kinds of fast-moving flying objects." She laughed. "Unless they're coming after me to sting me, but thankfully bees don't bother me too much."

"Oh, that's good to know. I don't want anything to do with a bee. I'm allergic. Daggummit, I was just sitting here thinking on the way over here that I'd like to live in the 1800s—you know, be a throwback to the wild days, but all it would have taken is one sting from a bee and I'd be a goner."

"Do you carry an EpiPen?"

"I do." He patted his pocket, where there was a red container sticking out. Looked like a toothbrush holder. "It's kind of awkward sometimes but out here I don't know what else to do with it. It doesn't go in my back pocket, so I just stick it in this pocket and go. So, anyway, you know where it's at. If it's not on me, it's somewhere nearby. All the guys know when I'm out and about I have to make sure it's close."

"I am so sorry. That would be really scary, and I guess I'm not helping by being horrified by the fact."

He shrugged. "I'm used to it. It's been that way

since I was a little kid. Got stung early on and if it hadn't been for one of the other ranch workers having been allergic…he ran and grabbed his pen—pretty much saved my life. After that, we always kept them handy. Anyway, you ready to take a ride? I thought we'd ride out in this bad boy and show you some of the cattle that you're going to be taking pictures of. It will be a week of it. Well, two or three. I'm not going to overwork you—you've got plenty of time. And like I said, when you go, either I'll be with you or one of the ranch hands, depending on what I've got going that day, but there will be plenty of room for Toby. I know you said he is four and that he's a handful, but we can figure something out. And if he's with me, I know how to hold somebody's hand and while you do your job, I can take care of him."

She slid into the seat beside him and he liked this. They were closer than when they were in the truck. Their elbows could touch; he didn't move his elbow enough to do it but if he wanted to, he could. He grinned at her. "All right, hold on to your horses—here we go. This land is big out here, rugged. Lots of rock, lots of sage, prickly pear, mesquite, some jackrabbits. We've got a couple of mountain lions that run around, but don't be worried—they don't come too close normally. I've got my shotgun here if they do and my EpiPen, so we're good. But I would suggest that at night you don't go wandering around by yourself. Can you do that for me? If you have a problem and you get scared about anything, you just call my number and, darlin', I'll be there."

Daggum. He said darlin'. He needed to watch himself. It just came natural, the flirting part. He hated that about himself. Sometimes he was a flirt; everybody teased him about it, but when you hadn't really dated in a long time, the flirting part just kind of came out.

She smiled at him as if she hadn't heard the darlin' part, which was a relief.

"Believe me, I will be calling if I hear anything strange and I will not be walking around outside by myself. Although I have a feeling that the nights are glorious out here. I bet you can just see the sky—so beautiful. I love looking at stars. I'm kind of a star buff. My best friend—she's a science teacher to middle graders, and oh goodness, she loves the starry sky. She's always teaching me about the constellations. Anyway, one night, I may just have to go outside and look up, so I might have to twist your arm a little bit and see if you'll do it. You're probably so used to seeing the stars at night that you don't even care."

He laughed as they traveled down the road, dirt flying behind them. He was in his element; he loved this. He loved showing off his land. And they were going to see cattle in a minute that he loved showing off. But he loved a good night sky. "I'll tell you, on that, you and I are alike. I could lay out under the stars and just look at them for the longest time. I'm going to take you up on that and I know just where to take you so you can see them. Here on the ranch you can see them well, but there's still a little bit of light twinkling in, if you know what I mean. And when the little bit of light comes in, it diminishes them somewhat. Because it's so dark out here, you think you're seeing all of it but I'll show you one night—we'll go to the cliff and I'll show you."

She stared at him, a serious look on her face. "You're just scaring me, Levi Tanner. You and I have a lot in common, it seems like."

He cocked his head to the side, hung his hand over the steering wheel, and gave her a little grin. "I guess. Is that a bad thing?"

Her pretty eyes dug into him, made his stomach wobble and his toes curl up. It was a good feeling.

"No, I believe it's actually a really nice thing. Means we're going to be friends. Which is kind of unbelievable, seeing the way that we first got to know each other, don't you think?"

He laughed and threw his head back. Then he grinned at her. "I think we're not supposed to talk about that first night because we definitely didn't have that in common—you taking those photos and me tackling you like a football player, if I had to, running your car into the water and having to pull you out. Yup…bad, bad situation. But me and wedding crashers do not get along. I am surely glad you weren't a real one."

She chuckled a little bit herself. "Me too. I felt so

sleazy that night. I'm just so glad to have that off my conscience. And again, I'm so grateful for this opportunity that you're giving me. It's just almost unbelievable. I was telling my mom a little bit ago and she couldn't believe it either, so I'm thanking my lucky stars that I met you. Well, I'm thanking my lucky stars that you chased me down and pretty much demanded you get that photo disk from me. Otherwise none of this would have happened—you would have just gone on hating me and we would have never known what we were missing out on."

Boy, she had that right. He had a stubborn streak in him and today he was very thankful for that. If it hadn't been for that stubborn streak and determination to take care of business and get that photo disk from her, he'd have just been sitting around angry about it instead of riding with her around his ranch, thinking about getting to know her better. Yeah, sometimes a stubborn streak could be a guy's best friend.

CHAPTER SIX

"That is one big bull." Rita stared across the pasture at the biggest, most massive, red bull. He had said what kind it was, but she had missed that; she had been in such shock, looking at the big monster. It glared at her from across the twenty feet that separated them. Her hand gripped the chicken handle—the handle on the ATV that she could use to get in or out of the vehicle. Right now, she was hanging onto it just in case Levi had to gun the gas pedal and get them out of the way of that thing. He was a leviathan.

"Oh, that's just Tiny. He's not mean. And we're

not selling him. That there little fella makes this ranch a whole lot of money. He's got babies running around all across the country."

"How?"

He stared at her, apparently realizing that not everyone was a rancher. "Well, um, we do a lot of artificial insemination. It's all about the genetics and he's got the best."

Her eyebrows dipped and her mouth fell open slightly.

He laughed. "A little too much information?"

She chuckled. "I'm getting an education."

"So here is the deal. I don't talk a lot about that black gold that runs wild under this ground and pumps cash into our bank accounts and makes all those paparats want to chase us around and get into our business. But that big boy right there, little Tiny, he's worth almost as much as that black gold is. Well, not really, but in my eyes, there's nothing better than a great herd and he's a champion herd builder. If I had to choose between the oil or Tiny, I'd pick Tiny any day."

Rita took in what he said. She truly believed after getting to know him that he could walk away from the billions the family had. She studied the animal. He was huge and she understood now, that as long as he could produce—and obviously, he could produce a lot of offspring—that people must pay a lot for the privilege of having a calf from him. Still, she made a note to herself that whether they told her he was harmless or not, Toby was not going to get near that animal or any of the others that they had seen. This ranch life took some getting used to. Tiny might make great offspring but he wasn't getting the chance to hurt *her* offspring. He was just too big.

And he wasn't the only one. There were a lot of cattle to photograph. From what he said, they had just scratched the surface of the animals she was going to be taking pictures of.

"So, really, were you serious when you said you want me to take a picture of their good side, like you want them smiling or something?"

His grin was big. "Well, I wouldn't exactly say we want them smiling. But just say for instance, if you were taking a picture of Tiny—not that he likes getting his picture taken; he gets a little irritated like me when it comes to getting our photos taken. But using him as an example, if you were taking his picture, you'd want to make sure that you show off his good parts, like how solid he is from his hips to his shoulders. You show that he's strong-looking. And you'd want all those muscles showing in the shot. And like on some of the heifers—they've never had a baby but people are buying them to carry babies, and the pictures need to show a good side view of their midsection."

"So what's bad and what's good?"

"Oh, okay, remember I showed you earlier how the cow was nice and wide, had depth, giving her a lot of space for carrying the calf? That's all important stuff, so sometimes if you take a picture from a bad angle, it doesn't show all the good stuff. By the time this job is done, you'll be a professional cattle photographer. You might not want to take wedding photos of bridezillas."

She grinned at the guy. He made her grin a lot. "Well, you could be right. I have taken on a few bridezillas before and they aren't fun to photograph nor their bridesmaidzillas. And I've had some groomzillas, too. But, for the most part, everyone has been great. Media just exaggerates the worst."

"Well, that's good to know."

"Well, I think that's because, Levi Tanner, you're a very smart man. I honestly don't know why anybody would marry somebody who wanted to act ugly like that. But then again, you know, there's always two sides to a story—like you and me. We definitely had our sides of the story."

"And there you go again, bringing up that night. You know we weren't going to talk about that and you keep bringing it up."

She could not help herself. She reached out and thumped his shoulder with her finger. "Just because I like to see you get all riled up. It's cute."

He hitched a brow. "You saying I'm cute? I'm not real sure I like that word."

She could only imagine that he'd much rather she thought he was handsome, good-looking or manly. "Well, sometimes you just have to wear the boot if it fits, you know what I mean?" She chuckled, and it might have been her imagination, but she thought he pushed his shoulders back and sat straighter as if trying to look anything but cute. She found it priceless.

He grinned, so sexy and his eyes dug into her. "Yeah, okay, so I guess if you think I'm cute, then I'll be cute. But one day, when I'm not your boss, I might want you to think of me as more than just some cute guy, you know."

Her smile dimmed as his words echoed through her mind. Could she dare hope? "I can't answer that question right now. But who knows? In the future, that might be a really nice idea since we do have so much in common."

* * *

Rita was going to enjoy this job. She had not really ever had the opportunity to live, even for a short time, in such wide-open spaces, and when she and Levi had ridden around on the property earlier that day, she had thoroughly enjoyed it. It was as if she could breathe easier. As if all the pressures and fear that had been weighing her down eased up in those wide-open spaces. And there was no denying that she had enjoyed spending time with Levi. Yes, it could end up posing a problem, but she would worry about that later. Right now, she was really thrilled about the job opportunity. About realizing Levi truly seemed to be genuinely nice, even kind. And listening to the way he'd talked about being a boss and having worked for others to get perspective…she had a feeling he was very fair. He had been with her. And right now, that was a very strong and positive indication that he was who he appeared to be. A good person.

He had said that dinner would be served at the chow hall, where the cook, who was a man named Scotty, fixed all the meals, and she was very welcome to join them for all meals. Or there was food in the cabinets if she preferred to make something herself, and she could use any of the ranch vehicles or his truck to go into town and get anything she wanted. He'd also invited her to the roping the ranch hands were having after dinner. It was just a friendly roping challenge at the arena they enjoyed in the evenings.

She decided to walk over and join the meal. She was going to be there for a little while, so she might as well meet the guys she would be working around. Plus, she wasn't that fond of her own cooking, so it sounded like a great opportunity. Levi had offered to come by and pick her up if she had wanted him to but she told him that she was very capable of walking over from the cabin; it wasn't that far a distance down the dirt road that they had ridden earlier.

It was a lovely evening for a walk. A cool breeze had blown in, a very much-needed cool breeze. Earlier, it had almost felt like the air from a hot blow-dryer. She had already taken her shower and it was nice knowing that she wouldn't need another one before bedtime. Then again, she had never been to a roping. She'd seen the arena was dirt and with the breeze, it could be dusty hanging around there, and she might get gritty. It was a two-edged sword, it seemed, but it didn't matter; she would take another shower if needed because the roping sounded interesting. And Levi would be there.

Most people would think someone who grew up in

Amarillo, surrounded by ranches and cowboys, would have been around rodeos and ropings. But she'd grown up in a small house with a tiny backyard on a cramped street with more small houses and cramped backyards. Dan and her in-laws had lived in a more upscale area, but they were accountants and not into anything that had to do with the cowboy way of life. She couldn't wait to bring Toby here, for the two of them to go on walks and to watch him play on this dirt road. He loved to play in the dirt; he was going to have a blast.

She was almost to the ranch house when she heard an approaching vehicle and turned to spot Levi driving toward her in the ATV. He slowed as he approached her, so the trail of dust following behind him blew off to the side before he reached her. *Thoughtful* was another adjective to add to the list of words that described him. He hadn't wanted to cover her in sandy dust.

Smiling, he pulled to a halt. "Want a lift?"

Her stomach fluttered. "Sure, I'll take a lift the last fifteen feet." She laughed and got into the seat next to him. He looked over at her and she was very aware how close they sat on the bench seat meant for two.

"You look like you're enjoying the country life."

"I am. Very much."

"Great." He drove the rest of the way to the chow hall and then parked in front. "I told the guys you were probably coming to eat with us, thought I'd give them a heads-up. They are all ready and are probably going to be on their best behavior. But I just need to point out that they are cowboys and, you know, sometimes things slip. Hopefully you won't hear any cursing or things like that but you never know. They're good, hard-working men."

"Hey, I'm sure they'll be fine."

"I know. It's just that they work for me, and you are a lady and I expect them to be on their best behavior. If you have any trouble out of any of them, which I don't expect, I'm just letting you know to let me know. Okay?"

"Okay. Thank you." She had a feeling that these guys understood they had a good deal and that they probably didn't want to do anything that would upset their boss or jeopardize their jobs.

When they walked into the building, the sound of

laughter and conversation filled the air. As eyes turned toward them, the room immediately went silent. *Talk about feeling in the spotlight. Wow.*

The cowboys ranged from all builds and looks and ages. And they were all looking at her. Wanting to put them at ease, she smiled and tried not to feel uncomfortable or intrusive. *Impossible.* This was their domain and she was the one entering it. Hopefully they didn't resent that. When they all removed their hats, Levi introduced her to each one as they passed and each one shook her hand and tipped their head at her. There were so many names she could hardly remember them all, but there were nicknames like Rawhide and Ricochet. By the time she reached the kitchen area and the big guy standing behind the buffet table wearing an apron and a grin, she knew he had to be Scotty.

He held his hand out. "Great to meet you, ma'am. I hope you enjoy the food—hope it's made to your satisfaction. It's just plain chow but when Levi told me a lady was going to be present, I tried to fancy it up a little bit. I added a few extra dabs of Cool Whip to my chocolate pie and made the tea a little sweeter."

The tough-looking man with the bald head and the big Marine tattoo on his forearm smiled at her and, to her surprise, seemed like a genuine teddy bear. She had a feeling that if he wanted to be fierce, he could be very fierce.

"Thank you. I love whipped cream and chocolate pie, so I'm sure it's going to be an extraordinary treat."

CHAPTER SEVEN

Levi enjoyed watching Rita's reaction to his ranch hands' reaction to her. They were good guys but they could be rowdy and he had given them the law this morning in a major talking-to on behavior that would be exhibited around Rita. In no way, shape, or form did he want her to have a bad experience while on his ranch here or in Montana. And his guys knew that he meant he would fire them on the spot if any of them treated her without respect or kindness. She might be a guest, but he was determined that she was going to have a good experience while she was employed by him. He expected it of his men toward any female but after what he had learned about Rita, it was all the more important considering her perception of male bosses had been so skewered to the bad lately.

What was wrong with men?

Sometimes he just wanted to grab them up by the collar and just pelt them one. Now, though, watching as she sat at the table beside a young cowboy they called Preacher, she laughed at something the kid said and he smiled at the sound of her laughter—light, airy, and happy. He'd gotten the nickname Preacher after he had revealed to the others that he had been a youth pastor for a brief moment in time before deciding to take up ranch hand work after the small church had hired a full-time preacher for the position that he had been volunteering for. He was a good guy. And he was looking at Rita like she was a breath of fresh air after a hot, sweaty day.

And that was exactly the same way Levi thought about her. And so did all these guys. They had worked their butts off all day in the hot sun and when this little brunette had walked in and smiled, the sun had cooled off a bit, replaced by a very welcomed soft and breezy atmosphere.

"I had a fairly sunshiny day myself this afternoon

when Levi took me out and showed me all the cows—excuse me, the cattle that I'm supposed to take pictures of. I'm going to have to get used to what I'm supposed to call all of these big animals."

"Well, ma'am," Scotty paused to put some extra tea in her glass as he strolled around the room, making sure everybody had what they needed, "as long as you take the pictures, Levi there can call them by the right names. I can tell you that those cattle don't know the difference in what you call them either. Just these cowboys."

Levi placed an elbow on the table and tapped his fingers on the top. "Scotty's right. You take the pictures. My job is to label them. But if you're interested in finding out their true names, you just ask me, and I'll tell you every time without making fun of you. Somebody who doesn't know cattle doesn't know the difference between a heifer and a cow, or a bull and a steer, or a Brahman or a Hereford."

"Well, I certainly don't! I'm already confused by what you just said there, although I do know that a heifer is a cow that hasn't had a baby yet, right?"

He held his hand up for a high five. "See there—you know some things about cattle. That's correct."

She laughed and slapped her hand with his. The touch sent a spike of pure adrenaline through him.

"I'm looking forward to learning more."

And he liked that about her—she had not put doing this out to pasture. "That sounds like a great idea."

She looked at Scotty. "Scotty, your dinner was wonderful. I loved the chicken fried steak. I don't eat a lot of it, but it was great—so tender. And I've never tasted mashed potatoes like yours. I could live off those, although it might not be good for my waistline. But goodness gracious, those were good. And I'm eyeing that chocolate pie, although I'm just going to have to eat a little piece because I'm so full."

That brought laughter from the entire chow hall.

She looked at Levi curiously. "What did I say?"

"You just think you're full." He chuckled. "Once Scotty puts that piece of chocolate pie on your plate, it doesn't matter how big it is—you'll finish it."

Scotty walked over and placed a nice-sized

portion in front of her. "I tried to cut it more to a female portion than what these fellas eat. I have to cook a lot of pies to feed this crew. They can eat about a quarter of a pie alone, each one of them."

She looked at the quarter of a pie sliced not quite in half, and he had given her the bigger piece. "Okay, I'm going to try. But from the reaction of these guys, I have a feeling I'm going to walk away from here really full."

"I should have warned you." Levi watched her as she put the fork into the pie and cut off the end of it.

She took a dainty bite, and everyone watched, especially Scotty.

"Oh, oh," she mumbled as the chocolate pie hit her taste buds. Her eyes widened and as she chewed, a smile bloomed across her pretty face.

"Scotty, looks like you have another convert. Now we better let these boys up so they can all go over there and get them a piece before they all jump up and try to take this one away from Rita."

Rita placed a hand on her pie and dragged it close to herself. "Not on your life, fellas. I have a fork in my hand, and I will use it." Grinning, she pointed at them and they all laughed.

Levi grinned. She'd known exactly the way to win friends in the chow hall.

* * *

Rita sat on a center bench of a metal grandstand seating area just outside the arena. Levi sat about a foot away from her, with his Stetson pushed back from his forehead and his elbows propped on his knees. Their feet were propped on the bench one level down from theirs as they watched the cowboys on their horses race from a gate the instant a calf bolted from a cattle chute. The cowboys practiced tossing their rope out and around the calf's neck.

She was enjoying watching them, but the scent of Levi's cologne was a tantalizing distraction. And she got the feeling that he was distracted by her, too.

This attraction was just such a surprise. She had never in a million years thought she was going to come here, to True Love, Texas to crash a wedding, steal some photos, and then be forced by one of the billionaire brothers to give the pictures up and then be offered a job. Then to be here with a life-changing job and a very unwise crush building on her boss. She'd never thought such a thing because she understood all too well that he was way out of her league. That was one of the many lessons she'd learned from marrying Dan, that she came from the proverbial wrong side of the tracks and, according to his parents, had never been good enough for him.

But sitting here beside Levi, despite the turmoil rolling around inside her, she felt at peace.

She looked over at him. "Why aren't you out there?"

He gave a mild shrug. "I am sometimes. It's fun and it's also a real practice. When we're herding cattle, being accurate with a rope when calves or cattle made a break for it is necessary. But this evening I'm sitting here beside my guest."

His words warmed her. And she knew, even with all the warnings of her brain telling her she wasn't good enough, that a crush was not a smart thing to indulge in.

"That's very thoughtful of you," she said carefully. "But I can watch you rope a calf too. I'll be fine."

His lips lifted slowly into a heart-thumping smile. "I can rope calves any day of the week but sitting here beside you is a treat that I'm not going to miss."

She nearly choked at his words, as a warm, sweet feeling curled inside her. "Levi, you do have a way with words."

His smile widened. "I'm only speaking the truth. I haven't had a pretty guest to sit by in a long time. And never one as interesting as you."

She knew it was silly, wrong to put too much into his words; he was, after all, a cowboy and they were known for flirting and saying complimentary lines. But, try as she might, she could not tamp down the pleasure she felt that he wanted to sit here with her.

CHAPTER EIGHT

"The calves are so cute."

It was a beautiful morning on the ranch. They'd gotten an early start—well, fairly early. He had picked her up at the cabin at eight but from all accounts, he had been up working since about six. She had gotten up, drank some coffee and had a piece of toast. She wasn't much of a breakfast person and after having had the massive, though delicious, pancakes the morning before, she decided to go light this morning to revert back to her normal likeness.

"Yeah, everybody likes the calves. Ours are really good stock and they grow into great steers. And the breeding quality is great. Do we need to move them around so you can get a picture of those a little bit better?"

She had walked around at an angle to snap some shots of the calves frolicking near their mothers. She had to get their tag in the photo and their body at a good angle, just like they had discussed the day before. It wasn't as bad as trying to get a crying baby to cooperate, but it wasn't easy. Still, so far, she had gotten several really good pictures. They had been at it for a couple of hours now. At first, she had been self-conscious, knowing that he was watching her. But as the morning had progressed, she had grown comfortable with it. She might as well—he was going to be with her a lot. But he said that later on, once she got used to it and could drive the ATV, that he could let her go out on her own. She would have a list of the cattle tags that needed to be photographed and that way, she could get the job done if he, for some reason, couldn't go along with her.

She actually enjoyed him being with her and they would come to that hurdle when they got there—on her roaming the ranch by herself. After she finished these shots, she walked back to where he leaned against the front end of the ATV. "That does it for this group. Where to next, boss?"

He hitched a grin. "Well, I'm thinking that it's time for a break. Been holding that camera up now for two hours straight. Does it make your shoulders get tired?"

"This little thing? Oh, no, it doesn't. Now, when you do a wedding and you're using a big camera, sometimes. But this has been easy. This is a smaller camera but it does a great job. Tonight, or later this afternoon, I'll load these to the computer and you can pull these up and go through them. You can let me know in an email what you like and what you don't like about them so I'll know as we move forward."

"That's a great idea. But sounds like it would be easier if we looked at them together. Why don't we do that over dinner tonight at the house. I can throw something together and we can eat on the patio. Bring your computer, or we can use my computer and go through them. Or I can come to your cabin later, and we can work on the front porch. Whatever you want to do—it's up to you. You call the shots."

She hesitated for just an instant. "Actually, dinner on your porch would be great. I know it sounds terrible, but I'd really like to see inside your house, if that's a possibility—just a brief tour. It looks beautiful."

He nodded, looking pleased. "I like it. My brother Cole did all the cabinetry work. He's really good. Although he doesn't hire himself out, he does do work for people who mean a lot to him. He made me feel kind of special since he did all the counters. You'll see—it's beautiful."

"That sounds good. I look forward to it." She really was curious about his house. And everything about him.

"Now, when are you going to go get your little boy?"

"I thought I could go day after tomorrow. Does that work for you?"

"Sounds perfect. I'll arrange everything."

It did sound perfect. He was handling the details

and she didn't have to worry about it. When was the last time she didn't have to worry about something? She couldn't even remember a time. "Thank you, Levi. Really. I appreciate it. Now, break is over, show me what lucky cattle are getting their portraits taken next."

* * *

Cole Tanner woke and smiled when he saw Tulip standing on their private balcony overlooking Kauai soothing blue waters.

He still couldn't believe that he was now a married man and that the beautiful woman in the white robe on the balcony with her cinnamon-toned hair fluttering in the breeze was his wife.

As the coffee brewed, he walked out onto the balcony and wrapped his arms around Tulip. She leaned her head back on his shoulder and he kissed her temple as they looked at the beautiful waters spreading out to the horizon.

"Good morning, Mrs. Tanner. I'm going to have to tell you every morning that I love you—maybe several times. I hope you don't get tired of hearing that."

She turned her head so she could kiss his jaw and her green eyes sparkled. He loved those eyes. "I guess we'll be sappy together because I'll tell you all the time too. Can you believe that we're really here, married and about to start our life together? I had to pinch myself this morning when I woke up in your arms."

"I can't believe it. And to think it all started with me finding a runaway bride stumbling along the road on a dark and stormy night. Sounds like a romance novel, doesn't it?"

"You mean a romance movie? Or have you been reading romance novels and I didn't know it?" She laughed—in disbelief, he thought—and his heart swelled with so much love for her.

"Hey." He laughed, full of joy. "I was a curious teenager, so I might have thumbed through some of my mom's romances. I'm really more of a mystery reader, but there's romance in mysteries, too, you know."

She continued smiling. "I'm sure you know love

makes the world go round. There was a time I didn't believe I was meant for it. And then you changed that."

He turned her in his arms so that she faced him, and his eyes dug into hers with the seriousness of the moment. "You should never have worried about finding love. You had some hard times, but it wasn't because you aren't lovable. It was because we were meant for each other. Thank goodness you're smart enough to be strong enough to run away before you made mistakes. I think about it sometimes, and how I might never have met you, and it tears me up. Makes me so grateful that I took that detour that night and found you." Cupping her face, he bent and kissed her—with all of his heart, with all of his love and the gratefulness that filled him and that would always be there that she was his and he was hers.

* * *

For dinner that evening Levi grilled steaks on the pit, his favorite way of cooking. He could have hired a cook for the house but he did not want people in his house. That's why Scotty cooked at the chow hall for the ranch hands instead of here at his house. If he didn't want to cook at night, he'd go over there and eat with the guys, but here in his house, he liked to grill. And that's what he did most of the time. Periodically, like yesterday when he had eaten there with Rita, he'd enjoyed it but he still liked having the privacy of his own home most of the time. And tonight, he was doing something he rarely did anymore: he was cooking dinner for a lady. It seemed weird to him; at his old age of twenty-nine, he should have been out there dating wholeheartedly.

Five years ago, when they had struck oil, he had been an active participator in the dating game. Then all the dickens broke out and he had become the poster bad boy—Jake, too. Them being the two younger brothers, they'd made blunders because they were still cocky, wet behind the ears, and fairly stupid, as their granddaddy would have said. They'd made a lot of mistakes and the dang tabloids had plastered them all over the place. They had been the "heathen billionaire bad boys" and there had been so much junk printed about them that it was just ridiculous.

Even now, thinking about it made him want to put a fist through something.

His brothers had talked him off the ledge and he'd had a lot of growing up to do. In the end, he'd had a lot of anger but his older brothers had a come-to-Jesus-meeting with him, telling him in no uncertain terms that if he didn't want the tabloids to keep printing ridiculous stories about him, he needed to stop dating every woman within a two-foot radius. Take a breather and start dating with purpose. Dating with purpose—that phrase had gone straight over his head. He hadn't understood it until Cole had told him to figure out what he wanted in a woman and then wait for the right one.

He'd continued the path he was on for another few months, full of resentment at having his life so uprooted that he couldn't live normally. He'd mulled over the meeting with his brothers and instead of doing what they'd suggested, he'd rebelled and dated a different woman every night. He'd danced at every dancehall in the Hill Country area and finally, on a night when he'd had some booze, he'd punched one of the paparats.

The lawsuit that had come out of that had cost the family a big fat sum and his dad had a talk with him. Told him to either get his act together and stop acting the fool for the tabloids or go find a job somewhere else. His father's disappointment had been what yanked him back from being a rebellious fool and to take responsibility for his actions again. Being mad that the family had suddenly gotten all this money and outsiders were taking over their lives—telling lies and some truths about him in the tabloids—had made him lose sight of who he really was.

Feeling pretty ridiculous, he had withdrawn from everything but this ranch. He had become a hermit for a couple of years; he didn't give the tabloids hardly a glimpse of him. He had made several secret exits on the vast ranch, ways for him to drive out of here in his dusty old truck. And he'd built ways into the other ranches that his brothers now used on occasions. He ate out at out-of-the-way places with tables near exits so he could fly under the radar.

These days, his brothers kept telling him he needed to stop hiding like that. He lived a boring life and when they spotted him, there wasn't anything for them to even make up about him. But now, Rita was here and life didn't seem so ordinary and boring. Yesterday had been a great day. He had enjoyed showing her his land and his cattle, and enjoyed having dinner with her with the guys and watching her reactions watching the roping. He'd enjoyed her company and same with today. And he was looking forward to the days ahead.

He saw her coming across the gravel yard from the direction of her cabin. His pulse kicked up just watching her. She carried herself with an easy grace that he enjoyed watching. Who was he kidding? He enjoyed watching her no matter what—she might walk like a lumberjack and he wouldn't care; something about Rita Snow just tugged at him.

"Hey. Getting yourself a good walk?"

She smiled as she reached the edge of the porch. "I am. I have thoroughly enjoyed my time here, just so you know. Guys like you who get to live this life all the time probably take it for granted but me, who grew up in a little tiny house and a little tiny lot of land with a little tiny yard—I'm loving this. And I can't wait to bring Toby here."

He set his grilling tongs down and walked over to the door. "That's great. You don't have to wait. I made some calls and we can fly down there tomorrow or the next day and pick him up if you want to. Come on in the house. I'll get you something to drink. You can put your computer there on the table if you want to."

She set her laptop down and then walked past him into the house. "You wouldn't mind going tomorrow?"

"Not at all. I'll call my friend Beck who has a charter business and he or one of his crew will fly here to our airstrip, pick us up and we'll go get your boy within an hour."

"We're not driving, you are chartering a plane to pick up my son?" The words dripped disbelief.

"Okay, look, I understand where you're coming from. Believe me, I was there myself. It took me a little while to get used to the fact that I can actually charter a plane and fly down somewhere and do whatever I need to, versus getting in a pickup and driving for days. It's different and yeah, it costs some money, but I can do it. And there's no reason not to. We'll do it and then we get back and you can do your work, if that's bothering you. It's much more efficient on you getting your work done by us flying down there, picking up your little boy, and getting back. Think about how much he'll enjoy that."

"Well, honestly, he's four, so he might really enjoy it… Wow, I can't believe I'm saying this but okay, let's do it."

"It's a done deal—we'll go pick him up tomorrow morning. Call your mom. How about ten? We'll head out, pick him up, take Toby and your mom out to lunch maybe, and then head back. We'll be back right after lunch and then you can settle in with him and then we'll get back to work the next day."

CHAPTER NINE

Levi picked Rita up the next morning in the truck and they drove over to the airstrip that was on the main ranch's property. The plane hadn't reached the airfield when they first pulled up and Rita watched as it approached, her nerves rattling a little bit. This was so new for her. She had to talk herself into letting him do this in the first place because that meant he would go with her to her mother's and that in itself was a bit nerve-racking. Still, it was what it was and it made sense that they would fly down there and then fly home, and then tomorrow she could start to work. It was efficient, with a high-dollar budget on top of it. It was the way the wealthy did business. And it was the way she was going to be able to, in the end, have her own business. The truth of the matter was that so far Levi had been so helpful that if he wanted to fly her out there, then she was not going to tell him no, that was certain.

"It's one of those little small Learjets."

"Yeah, Beck and his charter business."

"So they fly you wherever you want to go?"

Levi grinned. "Yes, they do. Reality is, though, I don't go that many places. I'm a guy who is pretty much a loner. I like to stay at my ranch. Sometimes a little too much these days. My brothers always tell me I need to get out a little bit more."

"Really? I guess you didn't strike me as the kind to be a loner."

"Honestly, I'm more of a loner now than I used to be. But, anyway, come on. Let's get out. If Beck's flying, he'll load us up really fast and we'll be in Amarillo before we can get our seat belts snapped on."

She laughed and hurried to climb out. They waited for the plane to taxi and then the stairs were let down. A handsome cowboy walked out onto the stairs and waved at them. He wore a T-shirt, jeans, and boots and a cowboy hat—not exactly the pilot she was expecting.

Levi walked to the steps and they shook hands.

Beck, as she already knew his name was, pulled his hat off, placed it over his heart, and held his hand out to her. "I'm Beck McCoy and we are glad to be of service to you today. I understand we're going to pick up your little boy."

"Yes, we are. Toby will be excited to be on a plane. As much as he can understand."

"Well, I can tell you when I was four years old and my daddy wanted to take me up in an airplane, I was gung-ho. I might have been young but I understood that we were going up in the air and I was all into that."

"Well then, maybe he will be too. I brought gum and that way if it hurts his ears or anything, he can chew on it."

"We also have earplugs, too, if that can help. But we should be okay; they're pretty good, pressurized. And we won't be up in the air that long, so if y'all are ready, y'all come on into the cabin."

She walked into the plush cream and white cabin

of the plane and felt so out of place. She had grown up with nothing—so poor she had sometimes not even known where her next meal was coming from back when her mother was at her worst. And she was just having to get used to having things since she worked so hard and then this was just a big treat. She was going to look at it as reality was going to come back soon enough, but right now she was flying with Levi Tanner and this was his lifestyle. She was curious about him saying that he was such a loner. She wanted to know more about Levi. And she hoped that maybe she would find out more about him as time went on.

They sat down and then Levi got her a soda to drink on the flight. Beck went into the front of the plane and closed the door; within moments, they were flying. Any nerves that she might have had disappeared as they crossed over the cloud barrier and everywhere she looked after that was just a beautiful white, snowy-looking blanket.

"It looks almost like you can just step out there and walk on it."

Levi leaned across her to get a better look. "Yup,

it does. I remember when I was a kid, I always used to think you could do that."

He smelled so good. There was no getting around how good he smelled. She liked his cologne; there was never going to be a day that passed that she didn't think about that scent and Levi. She needed to get hold of herself. He needed to lean back, settle back in the seat, put some distance between them.

But he hesitated and then he looked over at her. "You're not nervous, are you?"

Nervous about him being so close. "No. I'm a little unnerved about being here. I've never been in this kind of luxury before. First your ranch and then flying. I need to tell you right now—my mother lives in a really small house that's not in the greatest neighborhood."

"I'm not worried about the size of her house. Is she doing okay?"

"Yes. But it hasn't always been easy for her. She was a single mother with me and struggled along the way. I'm hoping if I can get a business started, she might come to live with me. I'd like her closer so I can look out for her."

"Well, maybe when you get your new business going, things will get easier."

"I hope so. That's my whole aim—if I could just get a start, I could help my and my son's future, and even my mom's."

He smiled at her. "Well then, we're going to aim to do that."

And just like that, it was so easy for him. Levi Tanner thought he could snap his fingers and everything would be fine. She wished it was that easy.

* * *

The plane landed almost before they had even had a chance to have a decent conversation. Levi had enjoyed the little bit of time that he had sat beside Rita. He liked her concern for her family. Like him, she was very family oriented. And he got the feeling that she had lived through some really hard times. Got the feeling that she was worried about him maybe seeing where she came from. Something was bothering her, and he hoped he could ease her mind. One thing was for sure: he wanted her to have a business in Fredericksburg and to have the opportunity for it to flourish. It was something he wanted more than anything he had wanted in a long time. He was a little baffled by his strong desire about it but if he was honest with himself, he knew it all came back to the fact that he really liked Rita.

Beck taxied into the airport, next to the hangar where their private car was waiting. Levi had rented a SUV instead of a truck because he wasn't sure how much luggage and gear that she would be moving with Toby. The black SUV gleamed in the sunlight as the plane came to a halt.

Beck came out of the pilot's cabin. "Well, like I promised, dropping you off and I'll be here waiting whenever you're ready."

"Not sure how long we'll be but you just keep the meter ticking and we'll settle up."

Beck laughed. "Well, when you book me for the whole day, I don't really keep the meter going. You can go spend all day here and I'll sit here waiting, or I'll go in there and get me a candy bar or something."

"He's really just going to eat a candy bar?" Rita asked with concern written all over her face.

Beck laughed. "No, ma'am. They'll have my lunch in there. I can go do whatever I want. Levi here—I just like to tease him. I'm not going far, though sometimes I do drive around or whatever…sometimes go see people or deal with my own business while I'm waiting. But we don't know how long you're going to be and I'm at your disposal, so don't you worry about me. I love this."

Levi shook his hand and they walked down the stairs. He placed his hand at the base of Rita's back as he leaned toward her. "You don't have to worry about Beck. He's well taken care of and we'll be back sooner or later—whatever you're wanting to do, okay?"

"Okay. I don't know why I was asking all those questions. It's none of my business, anyway. This is just all new to me."

"Well, the charter business is different. I book it for the day and he's ours. We could get on that plane right now and fly to Hawaii if you wanted to. We'd have to come back later—we couldn't get to all that in one day, probably, but he's at our disposal, so you think about it." He grinned at her. "You decide you want to take your little boy to the San Francisco Zoo, we can do it. It's up to you."

She laughed. "Levi Tanner, I really don't know what to think about all this. But I don't think I'll be taking him to the zoo today. Heading home is the best thing to do."

He shrugged. "I personally kind of like hanging out with you, so I don't care what we do."

She stopped walking; they had reached the SUV now. "I've been enjoying spending time with you, too. But I do want to warn you before we get out. My mom is going to cry when we take Toby. We had been living with mom for a while until I figured out what I was going to do. She's gotten used to having us around and she will miss him terribly when he's not here, even though it wears her out. And she worries about him. But, Levi, I don't want my mother or anybody else raising Toby. I want to find a way where I can make a living and raise my child. And this business that you're giving me the opportunity to have is the answer to my prayers."

Unable to stop himself, he lifted his hand and cupped her jaw. "And that's what I want for you too. Okay, I'm going to do everything in my power to give you a shot at having that business to where you and your little boy can have a life you dream of."

They stared at each other. His heartbeat raced and he told himself to pull back, to pull his hand away from her jaw. But her skin was so soft and her eyes were so big, he just couldn't do it. He did fight off the urge to lean forward and kiss her. That would not be good. But just for a moment—just in this moment—the feel of her soft skin and the look in her eyes was enough. Finally, he pulled his hand away and reached for the door. "So, we better go. If we're going to get you and your business up and rolling, we've got to pick that little boy up and get home and get started."

She paused after he opened the door and placed her hand on his arm. "Thank you, Levi. I mean that."

He gave her a cocky half-grin, to lighten the situation that seemed so heavy, laden with gratitude toward him. "I'm just glad I can help. Now, let's go get that boy."

* * *

Rita got out of the car the moment they pulled into the driveway of her mother's small white-framed house. She was ready to see her boy. The screen door opened, and Toby barreled down the steps on his little legs. Her mother came to the door behind him. Rita knelt and threw her arms wide, and Toby threw himself into her arms. He loved doing this. Hugging after not having seen her for a day or so was a huge deal to Toby. He screamed, "Mommy!" all the way from the doorsteps until he reached her arms.

She closed her arms around him, hugged him tight and kissed his temple. Her heart clenched with love. Never, ever could she love anything or anyone as deeply as she loved this child. Of course, she hoped one day to find a man she could love but that would be a while. She hadn't had any inclination to make that a possibility since she had dealt with Toby's daddy. Dan had almost ruined her for ever trusting anyone, but she hoped to overcome her fear and trepidation and hopefully she could have a future with someone. She hoped to give Toby a family one day. She just wasn't sure when she'd ever be able to make that happen.

She felt drawn to Levi, as much of an impossibility as that was. And Levi was a whole new ballgame.

"I'm so glad to see you," she said to Toby, knowing it was time to change the direction her thoughts had taken where Levi Tanner was concerned.

Toby looked at her with big green eyes. "I am glad you're here, Mom. Who's this?" His voice was small.

She looked up at Levi. "That's Mr. Tanner or Mr. Levi. I work for him."

Toby eyed him with curiosity. He hadn't been around many men in his young life. Not having been raised by a daddy or a granddaddy on her side of the family and Dan's dad had passed away not too long after Dan had been killed. One more reason why Laura, her mother-in-law, was trying to get custody of Toby. She was grieving and thought Toby would help her. She hated that for Laura, but she was not planning to give up Toby. But she also knew a man in his life would be a good thing. So the time at the ranch would be good for him. There were men everywhere. And Levi would be with them a lot.

"How are you doing, little guy? I brought your mama to pick you up."

She smiled at Levi. He was trying but she could tell by the look in his eye that he hadn't been around a lot of kids. But he was doing a good bluff. She had a feeling that Levi could bluff his way through anything.

"Mr. Levi is going to take us on an airplane."

Toby's eyes widened. "Airplane in the sky?"

"Yup, that's right…up there with the clouds."

"Like a bird?"

Her mother came out onto the porch. She was thinner than she'd been just a few days ago and Rita worried about her. "Levi, this is my mother, Eve."

He removed his hat and held it in his hands. "Good morning, ma'am. I'm Levi Tanner. I'm happy to make your acquaintance."

"Likewise. It's nice to meet you. Are you sure you're going to want to have a little boy hanging around there at your place? Because I can keep him here."

"Mom, we already discussed this. I know you want to help but Toby's going with me. And you need some rest."

She felt Levi's gaze on her.

Her mother put her hands on her hips. "I know. I was just making sure Mr. Tanner here hadn't changed his mind. I can make it if I need too."

Levi smiled reassuringly at her. "Yes, ma'am, I am perfectly fine with having Toby around. It's part of the deal when I hired your daughter."

Relief relaxed her mother's expression. "He'll enjoy that. I'll just go put his things in a bag."

She turned and went back inside. Rita saw how slow she was moving and knew her mother was hurting. It would take her days, maybe a week or so, to get over watching an active four-year-old for a week.

"Grammy's been grumpy."

Rita smiled at Toby. "Grammy is just tired. She's not as young as you and doesn't have anywhere near the energy that you have. But she loved having you here. I hope you cleaned up your toys to help her like I told you to do."

He nodded. "I did. Because I can make a mess."

Levi chuckled.

She looked up at him and smiled. "Believe me, he's not joking."

"Think about my poor mother having me and my brothers."

"I'm sure she loved every minute of it and had y'all helping clean up at four years old also."

"Yes, she did. Then Dad had us on horses and helping clean stalls about that age too."

"You have horses?" Toby looked at Levi with big eyes.

"Yes, I do. And I can teach you to ride if your mom gives me the go-ahead."

And just like that, Levi won her child's adoration.

"Let's go in and I'll help Grammy get your things. And I need to pack a suitcase myself." She took Toby's hand and led the way up the steps into the small living room. The furniture was aged but clean, and there were colorful crayon colorings taped to the wall that Toby had colored. There were also a few pictures of her and her mother sitting around. A basket next to her mother's recliner held her knitting. She was working on a tan and cream afghan, and it was draped over the arm of the chair. She needed to talk to her mother before they left. "Toby, will you show Levi your artwork while I go help Grammy?"

"Sure. Come see, Levi." Toby crawled onto the couch and pointed out the pages that were taped there behind the sofa.

She found her mother coming out of the bedroom and they went to the kitchen where they could still see Toby and Levi but they had enough privacy they could talk.

"How are you feeling?" she asked. "Do you need to go to the doctor?"

"No, I'll be fine. I hate being fifty and getting so tired. But I'll be fine after I sit around for a few days."

Her mother had been a vibrant woman before she'd started having autoimmune problems. They'd found her a good doctor, who had her start a new low carbohydrate diet and taking a lot of supplements that were helping. They'd been warned that her immune system had broken down over time and it would take time to heal. And though keeping Toby was still hard on her, she did seem stronger and Rita was hopeful for more improvement.

"Have you had any more communication from Laura? I felt terrible not telling her Toby was here, but I was afraid she might take him for the day and not bring him back."

"I know. I felt bad about that too, but she's the one who is threatening to fight me for custody, so taking him with me now is the best thing. It's all going to be okay. I promise. You rest and don't worry about it. I'll get this figured out."

She hugged her mom, then they walked around the counter and she realized Toby was now showing Levi his pictures on the other side of the kitchen wall where they'd been talking. Hopefully he hadn't heard their conversation. She didn't need Levi hearing just how dysfunctional her family was. Her heart hurt for Laura and all the pain she'd lived through, but she wasn't getting Toby.

Rita had to find a solution and she prayed that a good career and a stable environment would be all it would take to make Laura realize she didn't have the law on her side in this case.

CHAPTER TEN

Toby enjoyed the plane ride home. They put him in a window seat, and he was just tall enough to see out the window at the clouds and the sky. The little boy talked excitedly and asked a lot of questions.

Levi laughed a lot. Levi was happy to see how Rita and Toby interacted with each other. She answered his questions patiently and it was clear she loved and adored her child.

After he got tired of looking at the clouds, he focused on Levi. Looking across at him, Toby scrunched his little face up in a serious expression. "I want to ride a horse."

"Can he?" Levi asked, looking at Rita.

She studied him as Toby looked at her expectantly. "If you promise he will be safe."

"Levi will be safe," Toby said, as if he knew everything there was to know in the world.

"I'll keep him safe. I promise."

Toby grinned. "Can I ride now?"

"Not now, we're in the airplane. But maybe tomorrow."

"Tomorrow. Yay! Mama, I'm riding a horse tomorrow with Mr. Levi."

"Yes, and I'm going to watch you."

He looked at her seriously. "Levi will teach you too."

She chuckled and met Levi's gaze.

She was beautiful, but he liked her patience and her determination. And while they'd been at her mother's, he could see that she was worried about her. She made sure to give her mother a big hug and made sure she had everything she needed before they left. She was a caring person and protective of those she loved. He liked that about her.

Right before they landed, Toby fell asleep. Rita leaned his seat back for him, and Levi got him a blanket. As he was placing it on Toby, Rita placed her hand on his arm.

"Thank you for being so kind and good to my son. And my mom."

He had been leaning down to put the cover on Toby and he was eye-to-eye to Rita. If he'd been bold and ready to run her off, he could easily have leaned in and kissed her. But he wanted to win her trust and not run her off. So he smiled. "I'm not a terrible person. I know we got off on the wrong foot, but I hope you'll look past all that and see me for who I am."

She smiled. "I do. I hope you're prepared for my son to idolize you."

"That sounds kind of fun. I'll be on my best behavior with that kind of pressure resting on my shoulders."

She chuckled softly. "Thank you. I never doubted it for a moment."

They got back to the ranch mid-afternoon and Toby was asleep in the truck as they pulled up to the cabin. "Do you want me to carry him in for you?" he asked as she unbuckled the kid from the car seat.

"That would be helpful. As you can tell, he's a growing boy and it's getting harder and harder for me to lift him out of that car seat."

He was very awkward as he slipped his hands under the little boy's sleeping body and lifted him out of the car seat and laid his little head on his shoulder. He followed Rita up the steps and into the cabin.

She led him to the second bedroom, where she pulled the bedspread back on the queen-sized bed. "Just put him in the middle. That way, if he decides to move around some, he'll have the whole bed to roll around in and won't fall on the floor. He might end up waking up disoriented, so I want to put him in here and I can come check on him more often."

"He seems like a good kid."

She stared down at her little boy sleeping so peacefully. "He is. And I'm just so grateful for this job, where I can actually get to spend time with him. Would you like something to drink? Do you have time to sit on the porch?"

"I would love a glass of tea."

"That could be arranged."

They left the room and she closed the door. Then they went into the small kitchen and she pulled a pitcher of tea from the refrigerator.

"You already have it made."

She laughed and her eyes crinkled at the edges. "I drink a lot of tea."

"Stated like a true Texas woman."

* * *

Rita carried her glass of tea out onto the back patio of the little cabin. Levi followed her. She sat down in one of the wooden deck chairs and he sat down in the other. She leaned back in her chair and sipped her tea. She watched as he leaned forward, placing his elbows on his knees and holding his glass in one hand as he tapped the side of the glass with the ring finger of his other hand. Levi had nice hands. She watched him tapping that glass instead of looking him in the eye. They were alone now and she wondered whether he had questions. She waited for them.

"I noticed your mother seems ill."

"Yes, she has Lupus an inflammatory autoimmune disorder. Meaning her own white blood cells are attacking her body and her red blood count. It steals her energy. And stress, worry makes it worse."

"I'm so sorry. Is she worried about you and Toby?"

She felt so troubled that, despite knowing he was her boss and she didn't want to tell him her whole sordid life story, she needed to talk to someone. "Remember I told you my mother-in-law would like to prove I'm unable to provide for Toby and then she could try to take him from me? My mother is very worried about it and trying so hard to help me even when she doesn't feel like it."

"And are you worried?"

She met his searching gaze. "Yes. At least I was. But, now, with the prospect of opening a business within my grasp, I'm not as scared. This is my shot at keeping him, before she starts to file to fight me for him. You know, these days grandparents have a lot of rights, especially grandparents of a deceased spouse."

His expression darkened. "I understand her wanting to spend time with her grandson but to try to take him from you? That's not going to happen."

Her hand had gripped the armrest of the chair and he suddenly covered hers with his and squeezed gently. "I'm even more certain now that we're going to make sure you get that storefront on the square in Fredericksburg and you have full-time work here until you're ready to do that. And the little guy's more than welcome to be with us."

She was so tempted to turn her hand over and grasp his hand, palm to palm. This kind man was turning out to be such a blessing to her. It was almost unbelievable. And though she had pride and wasn't one to take charity, he was making sure that this didn't feel like that. And for that she was grateful. She couldn't even speak; tears clogged her throat.

"The pictures start again tomorrow, and I'll let Toby ride on a horse before we go. Now, I'll get out of your hair—let you and your little boy relax. But we'll get back on the photos tomorrow and then next week we'll head to Montana. And that's up to you—but he would enjoy the trip I bet."

"We'll see how it goes this week—how's that sound? I don't want to saddle you with me and my child on the trip to Montana if it doesn't go as well as we need it to. It wouldn't be fair to you."

"We'll just see then. I have a feeling it will be just fine. And hey, this weekend, they're having a festival in town. Maybe you want to go? We'll take Toby with us. He'll get a kick out of it. There's lots of things to do for kids. I don't go there that much. They do a street dance in the evening, and during the day, they do all kinds of things like bobbing for apples and three-legged races and things like that. They do it every year."

"That sounds like fun. Are you sure you want to go?"

"Heck yeah, I'm sure. Who wouldn't want to go? I've got a pretty lady and cute little boy wanting to go—I'll be the guy to take them. We'll have a date."

His quick quip was so quick and matter of fact that it hit her—she wondered whether he realized he said they would just have a date. She decided he just meant it as a form of speech and it didn't really mean it would be a date—like a *date* date. So she didn't say anything; she just nodded.

He stood and removed his hand from hers before she had given in to the want to turn her hand over in his and hold on tightly. "I better get back to business. If I'm going to get the privilege of hanging out with you all day tomorrow, I've got to get in the office and do some paperwork. Dang paperwork—I'd be happy if it just did itself, but sadly it doesn't. If you want to bring him to eat with the guys tonight, I'm sure that they'd be thrilled. They might have him out there showing him how to rope a steer on that roping dummy in front of the chow hall."

"We'll see. I might do that. Toby will probably really enjoy that. And, to be honest, he hasn't really been around men that much, so I'm really thrilled to have him out here for a little while. The guys seem to be nice guys, so I'm probably going to take advantage of that as much as possible while I am here."

He tipped his hat. "Well, I can tell you that the fellas will probably enjoy him way more than he can enjoy them. So I'll see you at dinner."

And then he was gone. She sat there, staring out across the pasture after he stepped off the deck and walked around the side of the house, headed toward his truck. *How had she ever gotten this lucky?*

* * *

In the morning after breakfast Levi put Toby on his horse and led him around the riding pen several times. Toby grinned the entire time and Rita took a lot of photos. Afterwards they loaded into the ATV and went out into the pastures taking photos of cattle. They found ones that needed to have pictures taken, and Levi had a couple of guys on horseback ready to help cut them out of the herd so Rita could get a better shot of them.

Toby—the little kid was cute. He had thoroughly enjoyed his dinner the night before. All the cowboys had gathered around him and teased him and had him giggling; he had taken to them like they were the best thing since candy. It was easy to see he was starved for male interaction. Levi realized, growing up, that he had taken having his dad around for granted. His dad had taught him so much growing up and he'd never given serious thought to growing up without his dad. However, as he watched Preacher showing Toby how to hold a lariat in his hand so he could throw a loop around the cow's neck, it was fun. The little kid never got the correct handhold on it but when he finally did, he was so proud, and his eyes shone brightly looking up at the Preacher.

And so was Rita. Her eyes just lit up, watching her son. It was clear she adored him. And although he could understand a parent who had lost a son wanting to be near that son's child, he couldn't understand a grandmother thinking that she would take the grandchild from the mother. Unless the mother was unfit and it was for the child's welfare, maybe then. But this was not the case with Rita.

Toby sat on his knee and had been helping him drive the ATV slowly across the pasture. The kid loved it. He occupied Toby with the steering wheel of the ATV while Rita walked around in the pasture, taking pictures of the cows the guys had cut out for her. Levi had never thought he would be a babysitter, but he was enjoying it. He hadn't thought about whether or not he had wanted to be a daddy, but as he got to know Toby better and better, he knew that kids were probably in his future.

This kid was great and he'd quickly become a fan, just like he'd quickly become a fan of Rita's. He had covered her hand with his last night when they were talking, offering her comfort. But he had wanted to gently turn her hand over so that their hands would be clasped together, and then he had wanted to pull her up from that chair and hold her in his arms. Whisper to her that she was beautiful and lovely and a good mother. And he had wanted to tell her how much he wanted to kiss her. Wanted to take her out and show her a good night out on the town. It had been a while since he'd wanted to do that, but he wanted to take her dancing. Wanted to hold her close. Wanted them to get to know each other better as they had a good evening.

While they were watching, suddenly a six-hundred-pound steer bolted and headed straight toward Rita. His guys yelled and both of them tried to cut the steer off with their horse, but it did a side step and came straight toward Rita. Levi held onto Toby with one hand and gunned the ATV. It lurched forward and the sound of the engine distracted the steer enough that it turned and fled the other way as he got the vehicle in between it and Rita.

Rita's eyes were wide as she looked at him. "I think it was coming for me. Thank you for being there for me."

"Yeah, they're unpredictable. You have to always be ready to run, or at least know where you're going to try to get if one does turn on you. He might have got spooked and you were just in his line. We don't know but it doesn't happen often. You okay?"

She nodded. "Thanks to you, again."

"Well, I'm glad I was here but I think if I hadn't been, you probably could have, like, thrown your arms up. Get good at this—throw your arms up and yell 'Get on!' really loud or 'Whoa!' or 'Get back!' But you need to make yourself big and loud, okay? Sound good?"

She smiled and his heart did a little jig. "Sounds

good. I'll have to test that out. If that's all it takes, then I might turn into a cowgirl after all."

He laughed. "I'm hoping that's all it takes. The last thing I'm hoping for out here is for you to get hurt."

"I'm not going to. I'm going to work really hard to learn the way of the cowboy."

He laughed because she looked serious, and he liked it.

* * *

On Saturday morning, Rita dressed for the festival. Or hoped she dressed right for it. She had a sundress that she had thrown into her suitcase for some reason. She had learned that you always prepare for something extra, just in case, and this was her "just in case" dress. She slipped on a pair of flip-flops, and dressed Toby in a pair of shorts and T-shirt and sneakers.

Toby had been admiring the cowboys' boots lately. And as he put his sneakers on, he looked up at her. "I need boots. Like Mr. Levi."

He had taken up with Toby right off the bat, and

his adoration of his new hero was huge. She had only been able to take pictures this week because Levi had pretty much been Toby's nanny—or nanny man or nanny cowboy. It was just so strange. She'd been hired by a billionaire to take pictures of his cows, and he was taking care of her little boy while she was taking pictures for him. She had been worried, but Levi assured her that he and Toby were having good man time. And it was evident that Toby certainly had been having a ball. And considering Levi was taking them to the festival today instead of hiding out from them, he must have been telling the truth about having fun too.

She had known Levi Tanner for a week, and it had been a week of miracles in so many ways. And on top of all that he'd done for her, he had also been a perfect gentleman. Other than holding her hand that day, he had comforted her after she'd talked about Toby remaining in her care, he hadn't touched her. Her other bosses had tried to touch her all the time and she hadn't wanted them to, so she was having a bit of conflicting emotions about the attraction she felt toward Levi. Because she'd liked him holding her hand and wouldn't mind if he did it again.

Of course, that was crazy thinking on her part. She didn't have anything to offer Levi.

The sound of the truck driving up and then a door slamming and boots sounding on the steps had Toby racing for the door.

"Mr. Levi," he yelled excitedly.

She followed him out onto the porch and saw Levi catch Toby as he threw himself at Levi. And Levi grabbed him up and lifted Toby above his head. Toby squealed with delight.

Levi was dressed in a T-shirt with the flag printed across his chest. He wore a white straw hat and as he set Toby back on the ground, he placed his hands on his slim hips that were encased in starched but faded blue jeans. And as he'd had on every other day this week, he had on boots. These were a little newer-looking than the ones he'd worn here on the ranch. He had said those were his favorite boots to work cattle in; they had been through the wringer and always come out on the other side. He'd had them re-soled so many times the shoe repairman told him that this was the last time. So these today must be the ones he'd said he was reluctantly breaking in to take their place.

She liked that about Levi. Just because he had all that money didn't mean he ran out and bought the newest, best things. He liked things comfortable—things he was used to. He didn't have the shiny new object syndrome. She had a feeling that Levi would also translate that trait into the woman he married. He just seemed like the one-woman type. Though, she'd read a little about what the tabloids had said about him in his younger days and according to them, he'd dated a lot. But the way she looked at it, dating was just looking for the right one. And maybe if she'd done a little more looking, she wouldn't have ended up with Dan. Then again, she wouldn't give Toby up for anything, so she had no regrets.

She got the impression that Levi was a man who would marry for life, if at all possible. She had wanted that herself but had chosen badly. Or Dan had just changed. She wasn't exactly sure which it was, and she'd never know. What she did know was that next time, she would pay extra attention to the important things. And right now, Levi was ticking off all the right boxes in the important things category.

Not, she reminded herself, that it mattered, because she was just here for a job and then they'd part ways. She had to remember that.

"You two ready to have a great day? I hear games calling our name," he asked Toby.

"I'm ready to win a big stuffed bear."

He had been telling Toby about the pop gun challenge of hitting the targets and winning a big stuffed bear. And that they were going to win Toby one.

"Then let's head out and win that bear."

They moved his car seat into the truck. Today, he drove a shiny late-model truck that didn't look very old at all. This was surprising because it was the first time she'd seen him drive anything but the beat-up old truck. He might have been driving the nicer truck the night of the wedding, but she hadn't looked out her window to see that night.

"Sounds like a great idea. I'll grab my purse and be right there."

Moments later, they were on their way, with Toby talking like a magpie from the backseat as Levi drove toward town. And Levi just grinned and answered every question her son asked him. She participated when needed but for the most part she enjoyed listening. She had to admit that this was probably one of the most anticipated days she had had in a very long time.

CHAPTER ELEVEN

True Love was a very small town. But being small did not prepare Rita for what she saw when they drove up to the city limits.

Levi could not stop the grin that spread across his face at her look of shock.

"There are cars everywhere. This town is a little speck on the map—where are all these cars coming from?"

"They just come in from all over for the True Love Festival. A lot of people road trip into Hill Country. And True Love has been holding this festival for a long time and it does have a catchy name. I might be biased, but it's special. We have the True Love kissing booth. I was the main attraction there one year when I was in high school." He waggled his eyebrows.

She laughed. "I'm sure you were."

"The high schoolers still enjoy hanging out at that booth every year, and it can get quite busy in that direction. They are basically the king and queen of the little parade that's going to happen here in just a little bit. And then there's the True Love Cowboy Bachelor Auction that actually has been postponed this year— it's going to happen at the Christmas festival. Not sure why they're moving it from this one but that's something they decided.

"And then there's the True Love bake-off and the True Love dunking booth. I've been dunked many times in that, too. And I try to avoid at all costs getting pulled into that scenario. I practically drowned that year. I never saw so many cowboys come out there trying to dunk me in that water."

"You went swimming?" Toby asked. "I want to go."

He looked at Toby as he backed the truck into a parking space. "Not in this swimming hole, Toby." He grinned at Rita and leaned across the seat toward her so she'd hear. "I thought it would be girls coming up there. But all my buddies and my brothers pelted those balls at me as if they were trying out for a major league baseball team."

"No, I don't think Toby or I want in on that game. It sounds rough."

"That is a very smart decision. Toby, we'll go swimming in a creek or the pool."

"Yay! I have to have floaties on my arms, though."

"We will get you some. And remember, never go in the water without them on. Okay?"

"Cross my heart. Mama made me promise."

"Thank you for telling him that. And you're so fun that I'm sure you were probably in that booth egging them on the whole time they were throwing baseballs at you."

"You'd be right about that."

"I don't see why any girls would want to do that."

"Most of the high school girls did it, thinking getting in that water was going to impress the high school guys who were trying to dunk them. And sometimes it worked—at least, it did for me once."

"Oh, now you're telling tales about your high school days. You dunked girls in there in order to get a date?"

"Hey, it worked. Sadie Louise Jorgenson went out with me once, then decided I was not for her. At that point in time, I didn't have any money. I mean, we were just poor ranchers—you know, trying to make enough money with our cattle to live on and to buy more cattle for the next year. It wasn't like after we struck oil. That got ridiculous. Nothing like money to change how people view you. It's really aggravating. Anyway, y'all ready to go have some fun?"

"Yes! Mama, can I unbuckle?"

"Go ahead."

They got out of the truck and then, with Toby walking in between them and each of them holding one of his hands, they went up the street and joined the festival.

First thing Toby saw was the stick horse maze and Levi bought a roll of tickets and let him get a stick horse and join the other kids inside the roped-off area.

Right beside the entrance was the funnel cake

booth, so while the sweet scent of vanilla and cinnamon wafted around them, they watched Toby race his stick horse around boxes that had been stacked tall enough for a kid not to see over the top but for the parents to be able to see the top of their heads as they tried to weave their way through the maze.

"So, you thought I was joking about people looking at me different after we struck it rich?" He was half teasing, but he'd seen the look on her face and was curious what she'd been about to say in the truck.

She tapped her heart and then pretended to play the violin. "I feel your pain, right here."

His mouth dropped open, not expecting her response. "Oh, you think that's funny, do you?"

"Hey, there are worse things in this world then having billions, you know. And yes, I'm just teasing you. I'm sure there's a lot of things to complain about, but I don't know if I would complain about too much money when so many have so little."

"We are grateful and do a lot of good with the money. We've also continued to buy more cattle and continue on to build our ranch so that we continue our ranching and keep ourselves rooted in what we love and where we began."

She looked so pretty today, and he was proud to be with them. He hoped there wasn't anybody here with a camera who was going to disturb them. However, he had already decided if he saw a camera, he was going to try to ignore them. He was tired of hiding out all the time and he had wanted to bring Rita and Toby to the festival.

He was just going to enjoy this day, because he was spending it with Rita.

He wanted to enjoy her by his side, laughing, smiling—and Toby too. They'd only known each other for about a week and they had to finish up the pictures, then go to Montana and come back, and get her business set up in Fredericksburg. And then, finally, he'd get to do what he had been wanting to do since the day they'd had breakfast together: ask her out on a date. This was as close as he could get to one, and he'd sneaked that in because of Toby and a town tradition.

There were a lot of things in life he was uncertain about, but one thing he knew without a doubt was he was falling for Rita and he was falling fast. And hard.

But he had to move slow or she'd bolt and run for the hills.

When Toby rode from the maze with a big grin on his face, they clapped and then bought him a stick of cotton candy to eat as they wandered around, checking everything out. He introduced her to a lot of town folks, but there were so many people here they didn't know that it was hard to find all the locals unless they were working a booth.

He won Toby a big stuffed bear at the toy shooting range where he had to shoot down three little monsters, but he did it and handed Toby his big stuffed bear. Then they rode the Ferris wheel. Levi had to check it out a little bit first to make sure their seat was secured well and the seat belt worked and the safety bar locked down. Levi turned to see Rita watching him with a smile and her eyes dancing.

"Thank you for making sure we're safe."

"My pleasure. I've grown very fond of you two and am not letting anything happen to you."

Toby sat between them and after they'd risen high

in the sky, she looked over the top of Toby's head at him and they smiled. He got the funniest feeling that she was thinking the same thing he was—that it was the perfect time for a kiss.

If they had been alone and if they'd been dating, that would have been exactly what he'd have done.

But they weren't alone or dating, so he grinned and hoped he didn't look like a lovesick fool. He was saved by Toby's excitement and his constant stream of questions about everything he could see down below them. He pointed everything out: the maze, the cotton candy, the petting zoo.

"Can we go to the petting zoo?"

"Sure we can," Levi said.

And when they got off the Ferris wheel, they went straight over to the small petting zoo.

When they saw the greased pig competition, he and Toby pulled on the plastic trash bags with holes in the top for their head and holes in the sides for their arms to protect their clothes. They had smaller trash bags for the kids and bigger ones for the adults. Rita held her phone to take pictures as they entered the pen with the little pigs. The minute Toby went to pick one up, they all scattered. He went chasing after them, and that was all it took for a Wild West commotion to break out. Both he and Toby ended up in the dirt, laughing together when they missed the squealing pigs, having gotten their hands on the animal only to lose it because they were so slick with grease.

In the end, egged on by the cheers and yells of Toby, Levi managed to catch one, finally! On his knees in the dirt and hanging on for dear life as the pig squirmed in his arms, Levi laughed. "Toby, help me hold on." Once they both had their hands on the greasy little fella, they grinned victoriously at Rita.

She almost couldn't take the picture, she was laughing so hard.

He had never realized that the cheers and yells of a little boy could dig its spurs into his heart and ride longer and further and mean more to him than anything he'd ever done. And then, when he looked up and saw how happy Rita was because of how happy her little boy was, well that right there did it for Levi. He was officially a goner, as these two had won his heart.

* * *

Later that afternoon, Toby was getting tired and they were ready to eat some real food, so Levi jogged back to the truck and grabbed the blanket he brought along. When he got back to them, he spread it on the ground beneath the limbs of an oak tree.

Rita sat down and Toby put his head in his mama's lap and very quickly went to sleep.

Levi headed to get BBQ. These people came every year and they had some of the best BBQ around. He was standing in line when he saw a very familiar face. It was one of the paparats who he saw often. The guy must live in the area because he was one of the regulars who probably made a decent living off all the different famous singers and artists who lived in the Hill Country. There were a quite a few of them in the surrounding area, if someone knew where to look. Levi glanced around, hoping that beneath some of these sunshades and baseball hats there was a celebrity lurking who was far more interesting than he was. This guy obviously knew where people of interest lived and hung out. But as he watched, he saw a little girl run up and hug the man, and a smiling woman joined them. Levi's spirits rose. Maybe the dude was here with his family and couldn't care less what anyone else was doing.

The guy disappeared sometimes and Levi figured he went to the normal areas—Vegas and Hollywood—and grabbed pictures of really famous people who could make a good paycheck payoff for him. Levi knew good and well that he and his brothers, most of the time, didn't pay as well as a famous person. The recent influx of lowlife paparats had come because Cole had messed up and started dating a local television celebrity and then broke up with her. Thankfully, it seemed that had all died down and he was free to move around with nobody bugging him.

He turned his back on the guy and headed back to Rita and Toby. If the guy had been here to get photos of him, then he probably already had his pictures anyway. He'd hate it if Toby and Rita showed up on the front page of a tabloid tomorrow, but there wasn't really anything he could do about it. He was done making a scene. He would just have to warn Rita of the possibility.

Carrying the BBQ, he went back and sank down on the blanket with his back to the crowd. His mood for the day was a little bit dampened by seeing the photographer.

Rita picked up on it immediately. "Is something wrong? You look kind of down."

"I just need to warn you—I saw a photographer. He might not even be here for me. I'm not arrogant enough to think that they follow me around all the time. But I just want to warn you that he is here. But it's a guy who lives somewhere here in the Hill Country because I see him at a distance a lot. I saw a little girl and a woman with him, so he might be here with his family. But I needed to warn you the possibility is that he's taken our picture. Maybe not, but him being around means there is a chance that you and Toby could show up in the tabloids tomorrow. I'm sorry about that."

Her pretty eyes held his and she smiled. "I guess payback is only right after what I tried to do to your brother. I can't really complain, now can I?"

He chuckled, liking her attitude. "I guess not. But what you planned to do turned out all right, so maybe this will turn out okay too."

"Maybe so. I can't imagine anything to do with me would cause a ruckus if I were to show up in a tabloid. Not that I'd like Toby's photo being there, but he has had that cowboy hat on pulled down over his face most of the day, so maybe his face would be concealed." She looked worried suddenly, then shook it off. "Nothing we can do about it right now. But I have an entirely different view from when I was taking Cole and Tulip's pictures. I would never even consider taking those photos now. Thanks to you and your education on the subject." She smiled at him and he smiled back.

She reached for the plate of BBQ that he had brought her. She opened the lid of the pack and made a noise of delight. "This looks delicious." She looked around with narrowed eyes. "I just realized that I'm going to have to be very careful with the sauce since I could get my picture taken with BBQ dripping down my chin and onto my shirt. Kind of like Tim McGraw in his song about BBQ dripping on his T-shirt."

Levi laughed. "Look in the bag. I grabbed a bunch of napkins just in case. Enjoy yourself." He scooted a little closer since he was facing her. "I'll try to block the shots of you. Though, I have to say, if I was the photographer, it would be your pretty face I'd be trying to take the shot of."

She smiled and his insides warmed. All he wanted to do in that moment was lean forward and kiss her. He didn't care who was around to see.

CHAPTER TWELVE

Rita had had a wonderful time with Levi. Sitting here on the blanket, eating together after they had spent the day playing games with Toby, they almost felt like a family. It was too dangerous for her to even think about, though. Everything about Levi was dangerous. But that's how it felt, and it showed her that somehow, someway, somewhere along the line, she wanted to have a husband and to make a family for Toby like this. He had shined all week with Levi around. It was so obvious to see that he craved more interaction with a male figure in his life. To be honest, she did too. But she was not the important piece of the puzzle here; one day, she would find someone who could be a daddy to Toby. But the odds of that being Levi were against them and she knew it.

It would be a miracle, actually.

When he looked at her sometimes, though, she thought maybe…there was more to this than boss/employee, or him helping out someone in need. When he complimented her, like today about being pretty, her insides melted. And there were a couple of times today she thought he might even be thinking about kissing her. She had been tempted many times, wishing, wanting a kiss from this wonderful, kind, thoughtful man.

When Toby woke up from his nap, he wasn't feeling well.

"My stomach hurts," he whined. He had eaten more sugar and junk food than he normally would eat.

She looked at Levi. "I was afraid of this. I should have called it quits before he ate all that cotton candy. And then all that funnel cake didn't help. I think probably it would be better if we took him home." She hated to use her child's illness as an excuse to not stay for the dance but she did need to get him home if he wasn't feeling well.

"Sure. I'm sorry. I wasn't thinking about how all that junk wouldn't be good for a kid. You can tell I'm not used to kids."

"It's not your fault—it's totally me. I was just enjoying him having such a good time—you know, watching him have such a good time—that I took off my mommy hat for a little while and just let him have free rein to do what he wanted. Which is a terrible thing but you know, sometimes you just want to watch them have fun."

"I understand. Come on. Let's get this cleaned up and get this boy back home to his bed so he'll feel better. Want me to carry you?"

Toby nodded.

"All right. You just lay there for a minute, let us get this all cleaned up and we'll be on our way, big boy."

Within moments, they had the blanket rolled up and he was carrying Toby out to the truck. They passed Jake on their way. He was having a good time; he had been at the rodeo area and he didn't even look as if he were worried about anything.

"Hey," Levi said as they reached each other. "Rita, this is my brother Jake. And Jake this is Rita. She's taking some photos of the ranch cattle for the sale."

She smiled. "Hi Jake. It's nice to meet you."

"Likewise, it's nice to meet you too. Looks like you've got a little sidekick there." He grinned at Toby. "How you doin' buddy? Did you have a good time?"

"This is Rita's son, Toby and he's not feeling great, so we're going to take him back to the house. It's been a long day for him. But he had a good time."

Toby lifted his little head and gave a weak smile. "I had a good time. But my tummy hurts." He laid his head back on Levi's shoulder.

Jake frowned. "Well, I'm sorry about that. I hope you feel better. Well y'all get Toby home." He started to walk away. "Oh, by the way, I heard from Cole they're flying in tomorrow. They had a great time on their honeymoon."

"That's a good thing. I'm glad. They deserve it."

"Yes, they do." Jake grinned. "Better him than me. I'm just not ready for that—not yet anyway. Anyway, I got to go check out these gals who are here tonight. I'm planning on dancing till they shut the lights off in the street and run us off."

"Warning—there's a paparat around," Levi warned.

Jake smirked and glanced around. "Then I guess I'll just have to smile really big and blow a kiss at the camera if he turns it my way."

Rita laughed. Jake didn't seem worried in the least. Levi needed to get a thicker skin like his brother; it would help him relax more, which he'd seemed to do after their talk.

"You do that." Levi chuckled as Jake tapped the edge of his hat in salute then sauntered off toward the music that was just starting to gear up.

"I like his attitude." Rita smiled at Levi, hoping to convey to him that he should stop worrying about it so much. I'm sorry we didn't get to stay for the dance. If you want to take us home and then come back…"

"Heck, no, this is fine. Let's get this boy home." He winked at her and she bit her lip as joy shot straight through her heart.

* * *

Toby was asleep by the time they made it back to the ranch and Levi was worried about the little boy. "You sure we don't need to call my brother Austin? Or we can just take him by the hospital. He's on, working the emergency room tonight."

"That's right, I forgot Austin was a doctor."

"Yeah, so we can just go by and have him take a look."

"Toby's fine. He just ate too much junk today. We're home now. And if he were to get worse for some reason, we can go. But honestly, he just ate too much sugar."

He realized he was a nervous wreck, worrying about the boy after he thought about all the things that could be wrong. "Okay, if you don't think he's having an appendicitis attack or something like that."

She smiled and rested her hand on his arm. "Thank you for your concern but take a breath and relax. Little boys' stomachs hurt from time to time, and jumping to the worst-case scenario right at first isn't advisable. We'll keep watch first."

Her touch and her reassurance had him backing off the ledge of worry a bit. "Okay, I'll take your word for it since you have the experience."

They reached the cabin. He carried Toby to his room and laid him on his bed. He stepped back and looked at the little boy as he slept.

"See, he's sleeping peacefully. He was just tired and on a sugar high. He had a great time," Rita said softly, standing close to Levi.

He could feel her hair brushing his arm and smell the sweet scent of her. "So did I. I hate it ended with him feeling bad because it was a good day otherwise."

"Yes, it was. Now I'm going to get him ready for bed and hopefully he'll sleep right through all this and be fine."

"Is it okay if I sit on the porch and wait in case you need me?"

"Levi, you really don't need to do that."

"But I want to do that. I'm worried about him."

Her eyes held his and for a moment, he thought she looked as if she needed a hug. But then she just gave him a small smile, turned and started taking off

Toby's shoes. Not knowing what else to do, he left her there and went outside and sat down on the porch swing. It couldn't be easy, raising a kid on your own. He never thought about it before. Not until he met Rita.

In a few minutes, she came outside and stood in the doorway, her body illuminated by the light behind her. She had a nice figure; he couldn't help enjoying looking at her, he felt guilty for thinking that when she had a sick kid in there. He was a jerk.

"Is he better?"

"He seems to be. He hasn't thrown up and he's not groaning. He's sleeping peacefully. So that's all a good thing. You didn't even have to watch me clean up puke. You know, that's not the most favorite job of a mother but somebody's got to do it."

"Yeah, I seem to remember my mom having to do some of that, and my dad too. I guess that comes with the parenting territory."

She laughed as she walked a little bit farther out onto the porch, pulling the door closed behind her. "Yes, it does. Funny thing is, when it's your own child, you don't mind. At least, most of the time. It would be weird if I didn't say when it's bad it's pretty nasty, but God gave us the ability to get things done."

"I think that you are a good mama."

She stepped over to the porch railing, wrapped her fingers around it and looked up at the moon. "I try. Thank you for today." She turned and smiled at him and leaned against the railing.

He rocked the swing back and forth methodically with his boot on the ground. He wanted to get up, go over there, and stand by her at the railing and pull her into his arms. Maybe she did need some comforting. He wanted to be the man to give her that comfort. And he wasn't thinking too out of line there; he just wanted to be the man she got comfort from. Again, it was a weird feeling for him. These were things he never felt before.

"Toby is lucky to have you for a mama."

"Thank you. I'm very lucky to have him."

He felt as though a thread between them was tightening, and it was all he could do to stay in that seat.

She had placed her hands on the railing behind her and she rocked back and forth on her hands as she looked at him.

He rocked the swing, holding her gaze and wanting more than anything to be holding her and not just her gaze. He stood. "I think I better head back to the house. Sorry we didn't get to dance but I'm glad Toby's feeling better. It's probably for the best anyway, the us not dancing. It probably wouldn't be a good idea."

He had moved to where he stood just a few inches from her. She looked up at him and electricity pulsed between them. He stepped closer, as if drawn by a magnet.

"You're probably right," she said, her voice unsteady.

"Yeah," he muttered, feeling as if he were falling into the pools of her eyes. He was going to kiss her. He needed to get control. "This…boss slash employee thing has its complications."

She nodded and it gave his heart a kick in the center. *If she thought it was a complication, then that was a good thing, right?*

"I better go check on Toby." She stepped back. "Good night, Levi. Are we taking photos tomorrow?"

"Yeah, sure, if Toby feels like it. No, if he doesn't. You just let me know."

"Thank you. It was a wonderful day." She touched his arm and there was a fireball in her hand the way it seared him.

"Anytime. You sleep well. And if you need me, you call me."

"I'll do that."

He stepped off the porch, almost stumbled off it but caught himself. He spun and strode to his truck. It took everything in him to get into that truck, but he managed to do it. Then he drove across the driveway and into the garage. He just sat in the truck for the longest time, thinking about going back over there.

That would be a fool thing to do.

Right. It would be, and he tried really hard not to be a fool these days.

CHAPTER THIRTEEN

Levi was driving through the pasture, snapping pictures of the cattle on his list. Levi had woke this morning not caring about tabloids or whether there was a photo of them in it. After he got back to his house, he had come to the realization that he just couldn't control what everybody else did. He and Rita had had a good time yesterday with Toby, and they hadn't done anything wrong. None of that mattered today. What did matter was that Toby felt better this morning and was having a great time riding in the ATV through the pastures with him and Rita.

The kid had fallen in love with cows just like Levi had at a young age. He remembered the feeling well.

They were going deeper into the ranch today. And

he was struggling to keep his mind on his business and not the pretty lady in the seat next to him.

When his phone rang, it filled the air with the sound and he wished he'd put it on silent. Reluctantly, he pulled it from the slot it rested in on the dash of the ATV.

He was surprised when he saw who was calling. "Hello."

"Levi, this is Virgil."

Levi had already pulled his foot off the gas pedal and was pressing on the brake. Virgil was the constable of True Love and wasn't on their friend list. If he was calling, it probably wasn't good. "Virgil, why are you calling me?"

"Well, it ain't 'cause I wanted to. I thought about calling Cole, but I know he's on his honeymoon and you know, after all that rigmarole with me throwing his bride in jail, I figured he probably wouldn't want to talk to me anyway."

"You're probably right about that."

"Yeah, well, I only have a few more weeks on my term as constable and I've got a little situation here. I was wondering, since I know y'all have done this before, if you could help me out?"

What in the world? "What do you need?"

"Out here on old Clauson Road, you know how far back in the weeds that gravel road goes before it comes to a dead end? Well, we got a horse, a mare, that's been terribly neglected. Somebody called it in, and I drove out here. It's almost to the end of the road. There's a new owner out here and he found it on his property, in a holding pen at the back of the property. This horse is not in a good situation, and I was wondering if you could maybe take it on. I called the vet; they'll take care of it but don't have any available space to board it right now. Can y'all give it a place to stay?"

If there was one thing Levi couldn't take, it was people who abused kids or animals. He felt like kicking somebody's rear end to the moon and back. "You bet we will. I'll get Jake, and we'll be right there. I've got to hitch up the trailer." He got directions and then he hung up. "I'm sorry to say this, but I've got to go pick up a horse that's been neglected. We'll have to put today off."

"I'll go with you."

"You don't need to do that."

"No, we'll go with you. I'll take my camera. I may need to take some pictures."

"Okay." It was against his better judgment but he wasn't going to argue. Good pictures might come in handy in this situation. They turned the ATV around and drove back to the barn. He hitched a trailer to the back of the truck. He'd called Jake and he was coming back from Blanco and said he'd meet them there.

It took them about thirty minutes with Levi driving as fast as he dared to. Toby sat in the backseat, buckled into his car seat, talking about them going on an adventure. Levi had explained to him that they were going to get a sick horse. Toby was all for helping it get well.

Virgil was standing beside a gate when they pulled up. In his late seventies, he'd taken the small-town constable job after a long career in law enforcement as something to give him something to do. Right now, he did not look happy.

Levi didn't blame him when he glimpsed the horse

in the pen. This might be the time Virgil was going to redeem himself a little bit. Levi swung his truck and trailer around, and backed the trailer up to the loading gate.

"Can I get out?" Toby asked when he parked the truck.

"Yes, but stay with your mother. I need to talk to Virgil."

"I've got him." Rita looked alarmed because she could see the horse. "You go do what you need to do."

He grabbed the halter he'd laid in the seat beside him, then jumped out and strode over to talk to Virgil. "She looks bad. It's a wonder she's standing."

"Thanks for coming out. If I hadn't gotten the call when I did, she probably wouldn't be. She needs some care and fattening up. She's almost a skeleton as it is. I don't know what gets into people."

"I don't either."

Jake pulled up beside Levi's truck, and his brother jumped out and jogged over, madder than Levi had seen him in a long time.

"That's pathetic. I'd like to meet up with whoever

did this and drag 'em through a patch of prickly pear cactus. Got any ideas who I'll be looking for, Virg?" Jake looked fierce.

"I'm gonna start with whoever owned this place before. But this land has been vacant for a couple of years, so that horse was put there just long enough ago to starve like this. I'm thinking somebody stole it and planned to come back and get it and didn't for some reason."

"That makes sense. There's been a rash of rustling going on, I hear, over in this area." Jake stuffed his hands onto his hips and studied the horse on the far side of the pen.

Levi knew about the rustling. They hadn't had any trouble so far but he figured they might need to start paying attention in case someone wanted to try to steal their cattle. Or horses. "All right, Jake, let's go get her," Levi gritted out.

Jake had had his horse in the trailer, coming back from whatever he'd been doing in Blanco, so he unloaded him from the back of his trailer in case they needed him. But they decided to go in on foot to start out with because the poor mare didn't have anywhere to run.

Virgil opened the gate for them. They moved inside with slow, easy movements, not wanting to cause the horse any more panic than it might already be feeling as it watched them from where it stood. Its ears had moved back and its coat was flinching. The closer they got, the worse it looked—nothing but skin and bones. The last thing they wanted to do was get her running too hard out of fear. They wanted to gently catch her and ease her into the trailer.

Levi went one way, Jake went the other, both of them holding their arms out wide at their side. Without even voicing it, they knew what to do. If possible, they'd get the horse to ease toward the open gates that funneled it into the trailer. But first, Levi took cautious steps toward the mare. He had a halter in one hand and he was surprised when the horse didn't move. It watched him with wary, almost pleading eyes. Levi wanted to throw up, he felt so sick about what had been done to the horse.

"Hey, pretty lady, we're here to help you. Can I

touch you?" He slowly pushed his left hand toward the mare's face, making sure she saw his hand. She snorted softly, shook her head slightly and sidestepped once. But it didn't run, either because it was too weak or because it was used to people and wanted to trust him and the help he was going to give her. Levi pushed his hand forward steadily and was relieved when the horse allowed him to place his palm on its neck.

"I think she's going to go easy," Jake said, relief in his voice. They both knew being scared would just cause the animal more stress.

Thankfully, they were able to get her in the trailer. It was clear that the horse was broken and had been trained somewhat as it let Levi slip the halter on, then lead her to the trailer and, with lethargic movements, walked up the ramp Levi had thought to bring in order to help him walk up and into the trailer. He had feared, and rightfully so, that it might be too weak and unable to step up into the trailer on its own.

Rita and Toby had moved to stand off to the side and quietly watched the horse get in the trailer. She had taken several photos. Her eyes were wide with sadness and tears shimmered in them. Virgil had gone back to his car.

"This is horrible. I'm so glad someone tipped the constable off to it. What will y'all do?"

"First we'll get the vet out. Jake already called her on his way. She'll meet us back at my place. And then we'll nurse her back to health. We've done it before for other counties. Virgil has never called us before, but I think this is Virgil's peace offering after what he did last time to Cole and Tulip."

"You'll have to tell me about that. I'm glad he called y'all."

They all loaded up and headed back toward the ranch. Toby asked all kinds of questions. Levi was amazed at the patience that Rita had. He had patience; he just didn't know how to answer all the questions. Toby might be four but he asked a lot of questions about the sick, neglected horse.

The vet was waiting on them when they pulled into the drive. She was new to the area and hadn't been out of vet school long. They were thankful to have her; the closest vet—Ash McCoy's clinic, was between

Stonewall and Fredericksburg. But over here on this side of True Love, there weren't enough ranches to support a vet. She made house calls, which was what they needed. Jake had dated her briefly when she'd first come to town. That had broken off fairly quickly. Jake had never said exactly why, but Levi had told him they needed a vet—Jake did not need to be messing up their relationship with the newest local vet. Jake had assured him that he had not messed up their ability to get the vet to come out. But it didn't take Levi one glance to see that there was a strain between the two. Thankfully, Hanna was more focused on the malnourished horse than she was his brother.

Once they got the horse in the barn, Rita held Toby's hand to keep him out of the way and they stayed back, watching from a distance. Rita was very curious about the injured animal and he liked that she cared enough to want to make sure it was okay. He and Jake and Hanna got the horse into a stall. Close up like this, it was a sorry sight. Hanna muttered under her breath as she pulled out a syringe and loaded it up.

"What is that?"

"Antibiotics and a boatload of meds. I'll be

coming out periodically to check on her, but we need to get her cleaned up. She doesn't have any cuts or contusions on her, so that's good. We'll just have to go slow with her feet and we'll give her some supplements."

"Good deal. Jake and I will take care of her. Thank you for coming."

"Thank you for being willing to use your ranch for taking care of animals. I've heard that you've done this before."

"Yup. We've always made sure that they know that with all this land we've got, we've got room for cases like this."

Her gaze went to Jake. "That's good to know. It's good to know cowboys have hearts."

Jake's brows met. "Sometimes."

She ripped her gaze off him and back to the horse.

Levi stared at Jake, wondering what in the world had gone on between these two. They hadn't even dated very long. So something was up. He was going to have to ask Jake about it, dig a little deeper. They didn't normally get into each other's business but something had gone on.

An hour later, Jake escorted Hanna back to her truck and Levi stayed with the horse.

Rita came to the stall gate. "Is she going to be okay?"

"Yes, she will be. It's just going to take a little time. Some special care."

"Can I help take care of the horse?"

Levi looked at Toby. "Yes, sir, you can. She's going to need some good care and some extra love and a friend. But, Toby, you can't come in here without me, though."

Rita gave him a look. "He won't. He won't be coming out here without me. So, it looks like this poor horse is going to have three caretakers."

Levi smiled at her. "I think that this mare is going to be a very lucky lady after all the bad luck she's been through. We'll do this together."

Rita smiled at him, even though, looking at the horse, there was sadness in her eyes. He felt it too. He was glad to know that Rita had as soft a heart toward animals as he did. Another good trait. She had a lot of them.

CHAPTER FOURTEEN

The morning after Levi and Jake had rescued the horse, Toby woke early and excitedly woke her up. "Mama, Mr. Levi said I could help take care of the horse this morning. Come on, we've got to go help."

It was early and she groaned, wishing she could close her eyes again, but he was too excited. "Give me a minute to get up and we'll go. I'm sure he needs you to help him."

"He does. He told me he did." His expression was so happy and full of pride and excitement. Levi knew instinctively how to communicate with her son. It was like watching a perfectly written movie script. She made mistakes all the time, but Levi just seemed so in tune with Toby, it never ceased to touch her heart.

They found Levi at the barn, just like Toby said he would be. He was tending to the mare, who looked so very wobbly. "Come on in," he said when he saw them. "Just move easy, little buddy."

She entered the stall first then let Toby stand beside her. She was startled when the mare walked over to Toby. As if she recognized that the little boy was not a danger to her. She placed her chin on the stall right in front of Toby.

"Toby, very gently place your hand on her—right there above her nose. If she'll let you, rub that soft spot on her. You can say something sweet to her if you want."

Toby nodded and very carefully placed his hand on the horse's snout. The mare barely flinched. "Nice horse. I love you."

The horse's big molasses eyes took the little boy in as Toby continued to talk to her. "See—she needs me to talk to her," Toby said over his shoulder, beaming.

"You're exactly right, my man. Your attention will help her feel better, eat better, and get well quicker. You're a good helper, Toby." He looked at her. "I'm really thinking she might have been around kids at some time in her life. She took to Toby so quick. She's still flinching around us."

Rita had the biggest urge to wrap her arms around him and hug him for how sweet he was to her kid. "I think you might be right. Not that I know enough about horses to know, but clearly she responds to him. And look at how she looks at him when he pets her."

"She knew the minute he entered the stable. I saw her visibly perk up before I even heard y'all."

"That's amazing." Rita's heart was full, watching Toby lean close and talk sweetly to the mare. "I think he would spend the night out here if we let him."

Levi grinned. "I think you're right. I think you two being here is a very good sign."

Rita's gaze held his, and she wasn't sure how to take his words. *Good sign for what?* The question hung in the air, but she didn't voice it.

Rita felt terrible for the horse and its condition, but she was so touched by Levi's care for it. And his care with her son. Every time he talked with Toby, her heart cinched tighter and she had to try to hold back any feelings she was developing toward her boss. But there was just no getting around the fact that Levi was a great guy. An honorable man. A generous man. A compassionate man.

She was in so much trouble.

Later, when they were driving out to take photos, he told her that Cole and Tulip had arrived back in town and immediately called everyone for dinner the next evening and that she was invited. She had tried to decline. But he wouldn't hear of it. He insisted that she come because she was his guest. And it would be good for everyone to meet her, considering she would eventually be having a business in town and because she was working for everybody for the cattle photos. Plus, he wanted them to meet Toby. He had a reasoning behind everything, but it was all geared to get her to say yes and go to dinner.

"But I was going to sell their pictures. I feel so embarrassed. And guilty." The guilt was heavy on her heart.

He placed an arm around her shoulders and tugged

her into his side. He gently lifted her chin so she was looking at him. "You don't need to feel bad about that. Let it go. You didn't do it and you had a very good reason for trying to get that money. I can tell you Tulip and Cole aren't holding that against you. Come with me. Face your worries and get it over with. I'm not going to leave you alone until you say yes. And I'm one stubborn cowboy. I don't know if you've noticed that yet."

Looking into his eyes, feeling his arm around her shoulders and the warmth of his body molded against hers, she was helpless to say anything but yes. Levi did have a way about him.

"I'll go. I do need to face it. And you are stubborn." Her lips twitched and his did, too. And then, to her surprise, he gently gave her a kiss on the forehead before letting her go and stepping back from her.

So now she found herself with Toby, waiting for Levi to pick them up at their little cabin once again. She had spent the morning going through photos she had already taken, because Levi had had to make a run to town and didn't want to go taking photos today. Plus, he needed to check on the horse. The mare was doing better, even after just two days. She looked as if she were making progress. The vet had come back out to take another look at her and give her another shot, and said things were looking good.

Toby stood at the window, watching for Levi. It was easy to see that her son idolized his new cowboy hero. And helping with the mare, which they had done again early this morning, only solidified the hero worship. She couldn't have asked for a man to be more of an influence for her child. She just hoped that nothing messed up the friendship that they were building and that when they left the ranch and opened the business downtown, Levi would still remember that there was a little boy who adored him and hopefully he would sometimes make a little bit of time for Toby. She couldn't let herself worry about that, though; right now, she could only worry about the here and now. She tried not to think about the way she felt about Levi. She couldn't let herself think about it.

Toby began jumping up and down, yelling Levi's

name, as the big truck pulled up outside. Toby raced to the door and slung it open before Levi could get out of his truck.

Levi reached over to the passenger's seat and picked up a big box and, as he got out, tucked it under his arm. He was grinning and her heart did that kick to the center she'd started to feel whenever she saw him.

"How's my little buddy?" Levi walked up onto the porch and scrubbed Toby's sandy hair.

Toby beamed up at him. "I'm good. Ready to go to dinner."

"Well, that's great but first I had to go to town and pick you up a little something." He handed the box to Toby.

Toby's eyes were wide as he looked from the box to Levi and then to her. "For me?" The awe in his voice was rich.

"Nobody else deserves it more. So go ahead and open it, son."

Her heart caved in at the sound of Levi calling her son *son*. And he had bought her boy something special. She blinked back tears. Toby had never gotten a gift from his daddy. He'd almost been killed by his daddy, though no one but her and her mother knew this. She closed her eyes and willed the emotional storm to dissipate. She silently breathed in and out, and when she opened her eyes, Levi stared at her with troubled, worried eyes.

She smiled. "Go ahead, open it," she urged Toby, willing Levi not to say anything about seeing her struggling.

Thankfully, he didn't. Moments later, Toby had the lid off. A pair of brown boots—much like the ones Levi wore and loved—lay inside the box. Earlier, Levi had asked her what size shoe Toby wore and what size jeans too. Inside the box were two new pairs of jeans and a cowboy shirt and a couple of T-shirts that had cowboy sayings on them.

Toby was ecstatic and squealed, then sank to the floor and yanked his tennis shoes off as he reached for the boots. Levi went down on his knee and as Toby was saying thank you over and over again, Levi helped him put the boots on. They fit perfectly.

Just like Levi did in their lives.

She ignored the thought. "Thank you for that, Levi. It was so nice, but you didn't have to do that. However, Toby loves them, and I can't tell you how happy watching him get so excited about them made me."

"I was glad to do it. I told him I was going to get him some boots. Now you're a real cowboy, little fella."

"And one day I'll be able to ride a horse. When we get Rosey all fixed up and healthy, you can teach me how to ride her."

Levi smiled. "So you named her Rosey? That's a good name, and I'll teach you to ride. If you're helping me with that horse and we get her all healthy and she's able to have riders, then she would be perfect for you, as long as I make sure she's safe and easy to ride. If not, we'll get you another horse that you can ride."

She wanted to tell Levi not to make too many promises, that Toby could get hurt. But she didn't want to say it in front of Toby. Maybe later tonight, after dinner.

When Toby was all decked out in his new boots and his new Western shirt with his old jeans—they opted to let him wait until she washed his new jeans because they were scratchy—they headed out to Cole and Tulip's ranch, which was not too far down the road. Rita fought down her nerves. It was over and she hadn't let herself sell the pictures and they just had to move forward. And she could tell from just being at the wedding that Tulip and Cole were great people. They had talked to everyone and been so down-to-earth that she had hated the thought of selling them out, but it had meant hopefully getting a life with Toby and herself and that had trumped everything. She decided that she could edit the photos and give them to the couple to make up for what she'd almost done.

As they got out and were about to go in, Levi reached down and took her hand. Toby walked ahead of them. She looked at Levi, uncertain why he was holding her hand. Part of her wanted him to hold her hand and never let go but the reasonable, smart part of her knew not to get her hopes up.

"Relax." He squeezed her hand and she realized he was just being a friend.

She nodded and squeezed his hand back. "I'm trying. It's a good time to face them."

"Come on, everything's going to be okay. They already know and they're fine with it. They probably won't even mention it."

"But I will. I have to. I have to tell them I'm sorry that I almost did that."

"Whatever you think. But it's not necessary." As he pushed the door open, he let go of her hand and let her walk ahead of him.

They were greeted by a bunch of smiling faces. Tulip came forward, beautiful and happy and with a huge ring sparkling on her finger. "Hi. I'm Tulip—'course, you already know that—but we are so glad to have you in our home." And with that, she hugged Rita.

Rita hugged her back, blushing because she was so embarrassed. "Thank you for having me, and I'm so sorry."

Tulip looked into her eyes. "Don't apologize. You did what you thought you needed to do and even if you had sold the pictures, we would have lived through it. We hear that you have been doing a fantastic job taking pictures of cattle for Cole and his brothers. We appreciate you more than you know." Then she bent down and held her hand out to Toby. "Hi, I'm Tulip."

Toby grinned at her. "I'm Toby and your name is a flower."

"Yes, it is. I hear you're helping take care of the sick mare they found who needed a lot of love. Levi says you're her buddy."

Toby beamed. "She's my buddy. And look—I got some new boots Mr. Levi gave me. Aren't they good? They're for becoming a cowboy like him."

"Perfect. He's a good cowboy to be like, and he's very proud of you."

Rita was so very happy Levi had busted in her room that night and stopped her from making a huge mistake.

Everybody was so welcoming, including his

mother and dad, and as the evening flew by, she envied them. Not for their money but for their amazing closeness and giving spirits.

Her thoughts went to Dan and her in-laws, who'd been cold and never wanted their son to marry her. Had always thought they were better than her and her mother, and that their son could do no wrong.

Oh, how wrong they'd been.

CHAPTER FIFTEEN

After everyone left, Tulip was wiping down the kitchen counter, feeling so very happy. She and Cole had had a marvelous, wonderful honeymoon but now they were home and she was so eager to begin their lives together that she hadn't even minded coming back to reality. And tonight, deciding to throw an impromptu dinner party because Cole's mother and father were still in town after coming in for the wedding but would be leaving tomorrow to visit friends. She'd also invited all the brothers over, had been fun. She had loved being here in Cole's house—*their* house—entertaining.

Her mother had been invited, too, but Mira had gone to Hot Springs with a group of ladies and they were having a ball seeing the sights and spending some time at the spas. They loved that town and tried to do that trip once a year. So she hadn't gotten to come. Tulip would see her soon, though; they planned to go out for lunch when Mira got back and she'd tell her all about the honeymoon.

Cole's mother was loading the dishwasher. Rita had tried to help but they had told her to take that sleepy little boy home and put him to bed, that they could take care of the kitchen, and so she had left with Levi. They all watched them walk down the hallway, with Levi carrying the darling little boy, whose head rested on Levi's shoulder. Levi's expression through the whole evening had been interesting.

Now, as Tulip folded the towel she had been using to wipe the counter, she leaned her back against it and met Barbara's gaze. "It was a great evening, don't you think?"

"I thought it was fantastic, and thank you so much for doing it. We miss our boys. We are really happy to see Cole so happy and you sparkle. We are thrilled you are a part of the family and that you'll be here enjoying this ranch with Cole. And I cannot tell you again and again how beautiful the yard looks after you worked so hard on it. It's just amazing. Honestly, I worried when I left that it was just going to go down the tubes, but you came along and everything blossomed, including my son. Thank you."

Tulip was delighted. "I'm blessed to be here. God truly led me to your son. The flowers were a bonus."

"I agree. And speaking about happiness, did you notice Levi tonight? He was enthralled." Barbara said the words slowly and with wonder.

"I noticed that too. Enthralled, captivated—he couldn't take his eyes off Rita. And the way he and Toby get along is just beautiful. You can easily tell that that little boy adores him."

"I wonder if they're in love. They look like it."

Tulip heard the anticipation and hope in her words. "It will be exciting to see where this goes after they make the trip out to Montana to take photos. I think love is in the air."

Cole's mother smiled. "I would be thrilled. I don't say it very often, but I am looking forward to this family growing and grandchildren. Although we're traveling a lot, our plan is to do what we want to do now but when my grandbabies start showing up, I'm going to be around. And no, don't worry—I'm not going to come back here and take over this big house. We're going to build us something smaller and leave this to you and Cole, so make it your own, dear. I'm hoping you fill it up with love and small feet racing around."

"Thank you." Tulip's heart warmed. "We want lots of children. We're just enjoying each other for a little while but believe me, you and my mother are on the same page. I have a feeling that the two of you are going to love each other. I know that you got to meet Mom at the wedding but it will be nice when she's able to come over and just visit. She went on that Hot Springs trip—she and her gals from the salon, they just love that trip every year. I think she'll be spending more time over here when the babies come eventually."

They smiled at each other, finished the kitchen

and then both of them headed out to meet the guys before they all turned in for bed.

Tulip walked over to Cole, who stood by the outdoor fireplace, talking to his dad. He opened his arms; she walked into them and hugged him, and laid her head on his chest.

He kissed the top of her head. "Thank you for a beautiful evening. You did a great job entertaining everyone and the meal was amazing."

She looked up at him. "I loved it. I loved everything about it." And she did.

CHAPTER SIXTEEN

The day after they'd had dinner at Cole's, Levi was working with the mare before he headed out to take Toby and Rita back out to take more photos. Rita had taken Toby back to the ranch house to grab some breakfast and get him ready for the day.

Jake strolled in, a folded magazine under his arm. "How's the mare doing this morning?"

"Doing better. She's getting stronger every day. She still has a long road to go but the antibiotics are working, and the vitamins, too. What is that under your arm?"

Jake grinned. "Well, you know, you didn't say anything at dinner last night and I was really curious about that since you're usually on the road every morning, going and checking out the tabloids when you make your run. Anyway, you made the tabloids two mornings in a row. You're the reckless Tanner boy who's found love. Maybe there's one down and more to go, and you're the next in line is what they're speculating."

Jake held out two tabloids—one from the day before and one from that morning. Sure enough, the tabloids had a photo of him and Rita and Toby on the first one, him holding Toby and speculating that he'd found love. And then today's was another one from the same event; he and Rita stood close and talked in one photo and in the next photo, they sat on the blanket together while Toby had his head in his mother's lap, sleeping. They looked happy. He grinned, thinking about that day. He had had a wonderful time.

"Are you grinning?"

Levi looked up from the tabloid. "Yeah, I am. It's a good picture, don't you think?"

Jake laughed. "Well, yeah, they are good pictures but they're about you. You don't normally smile when you look at a tabloid—you just, like, scowl and get all hot and bothered and storm out angry, wanting to take on the world and fight like a maniac."

"Yeah, I know, but well, this…this is not important. And, to be honest, it might be true."

Jake gawked at him. "Seriously? I kind of was wondering. Y'all really looked close last night. You were looking at her like you were thinking she was the best thing since banana splits and she was looking at you like you were, too, so I kind of thought that was something special."

"Oh, yeah, it is. It's kind of weird, though. I'm not used to feeling like this and I'm thinking it might not be true and it might go away and that won't feel really good."

"I hear you. I'm amazed that you're saying what you're saying. I don't know…I figured you'd be the last of us to get hooked and drawn in by love and marriage."

"Well, I kind of was thinking that, too, but I don't know. There's just something about Rita that I can't shake. I want to be around her all the time. It's been that way since I first laid eyes on her at the dance, even though she was a wedding crasher and I thought I was despising her. I couldn't help myself. I guess there is something to that when you meet someone who's going to be special in your life, you sometimes kind of know it and, well, that's how I feel. And these tabloids, they're only saying the truth. They aren't saying something terrible and untrue and ugly. Oh, they have before, but not this time. I'm hoping it will just go away, but right now, I can't be angry about that."

"Well, buddy, I'd say you've come a long way. And good luck with that."

Levi heaved in a deep breath. "Thanks. I'm moving real slow, though. I don't want to run her off."

"That's probably for the best—slow and easy is better than fast and furious and taking a chance of running her off."

"And Toby...I don't want to, you know, take a chance of hurting Toby. He's very tender and he hasn't been around guys very much, so he kind of idolizes me. It feels pretty good but I don't want to do anything that messes with his little head, you know what I mean? I want to just be a good thing in his life. I don't want something to happen between me and Rita and then him not get to see me anymore, you know? I hope if something were to happen, and me and Rita aren't together in the end, at least me and Toby will have a lasting relationship."

"Man, you've got it bad."

"Yup, I do."

* * *

On Monday, they climbed into the jet to fly to Montana. Toby clutched a small insulated lunch kit in his hand that Scotty had prepared for him that morning. Scotty enjoyed fixing Toby treats. Rita had peeked into the container and saw that it was packed with three different sandwich-sized containers of various kinds of cookies that Toby loved. Twice that week, when she had gone out to take pictures with Levi for the morning, Toby had stayed behind with Scotty to bake cookies. The older man had been thrilled to have company in the kitchen and really enjoyed the little boy helping out. He had a grandson of his own who he was going to go visit in a couple of weeks, and Rita had grown quickly to adore Scotty.

Toby grinned at Levi. "I wish Scotty could come with us."

"But if Scotty was with us, who would feed the cowboys?"

Toby took that in with a serious expression. "Yeah, they need Scotty. I'll see him when we get back. And I have cookies."

"I may have to try to steal a cookie from you."

"You can. Mama can too. He gave me lots."

Levi's gaze met hers from across the short aisle. The seats faced each other and their knees were not too far apart; if he stretched out his legs, they would be beside hers.

"And I brought you some coloring books, so if you want them, they're in this little backpack right here." She sat the little backpack in the seat with Toby, and he immediately unzipped it and pulled one out. It was of cowboys and horses and cows and some farm animals thrown in.

"Cool. Thank you, Mama."

She watched him color as the plane was taking off. She still marveled at this lifestyle, with private jets and limousines and tabloids. She had seen the tabloids yesterday afternoon when she'd gone to the store to pick up coloring books and other supplies for Toby and them for the trip. Levi had watched Toby and they looked after the mare while she ran her errands.

She had spotted them in the pictures the moment she'd gotten in line with her items. Shock rocked through her at first when she saw them standing by the maze together, waiting on Toby. But the picture of them from another angle actually made it look as if he was about to kiss her. As a photographer herself, she knew the photographer had been standing at the right angle and when Levi had leaned toward her while they were talking, the shot was just the perfect angle to be an optical illusion. The viewers' eyes and imagination and the headline also helped paint the lie. *Wild boy Levi Tanner finds love at last at the local festival.* She cringed and wondered what Levi would think and looked around to see no one was paying any attention to her and would probably not recognize her.

Except the older woman working the register. Her eyes brightened as Rita placed her items on the counter.

"You and Levi look really happy in that photo. That Levi hasn't been in lately. He used to come in here almost every week to see if there was anything about him on the front page. He hates them. When he didn't come in to check them out, I thought he might be sick or something. Then Jake came in and picked some up, so I know he knows. Poor guy. They used to spread all kinds of rumors about him. He stays out at his ranch most of the time these days, so it's hard for them to get a shot of him and a woman on the cover. It's been a while. But he gets mad when his brothers are on there too."

She rambled on as Rita tried to make sense of all of this. *Levi knew they were on the cover and he hadn't said anything?*

She was thankful no one was behind her in the line to hear the conversation. "Well, they do spread rumors. For instance, I just work for him, and he took me and my son to the festival. We were waiting for him to come out of the maze in that photo. We were not having a kiss. The photographer made it look like we were kissing. Those are lies."

"Well, that's a shame. You look nice, and I think that young man needs a good woman in his life. Lies, all of it, but I carry them because they sell."

She had been thinking about that encounter since leaving the store, and she had an odd feeling in her gut about him not mentioning the pictures. He didn't even seem upset. *What was up with that?* He'd been furious about tabloids but now it was as if this story about her and him didn't matter. *What did that mean?* At one point in time, they had just spread terrible lies about Levi when he was younger and much less mature enough to handle such things. *Had he now decided it didn't matter?*

"Are you ready for a fun week?" he asked, watching her.

"Doing what?" she asked, not focused.

"Exploring the ranch."

"Oh, yes, right. I guess we'll do it in a truck?"

His gaze dug deeper. "Some of it. And some of it

we'll do in a helicopter. It's a lot of land to cover, so I hired a pilot. We'll fly over several areas and if we see something we really want to take a picture of, we'll drop down and take it. But some of it we'll do in the truck."

A helicopter. She hadn't realized that. Again, so many different things to wonder about in this lifestyle. "Is that a normal thing?"

"On big ranches, yeah. I mean, some places they even herd cattle with helicopters. I don't like to do it. I don't want to scare the cattle. But we're not going to be herding any cattle; we're just going to be checking things out. But it comes in handy. Sometimes it has to be done. Are you distracted about something?" He glanced at Toby as if to make sure he wasn't paying attention to their conversation.

"No, I'm okay." She nodded, trying to convey she was fine without saying anything to draw Toby's attention.

"You sure?"

She nodded. "I'm sure." Even if she planned to talk to him about the tabloids, now was not the time.

They spent the rest of the trip talking about ranching, and Toby had a lot of questions that Levi was patiently answering. Half the time, Rita just listened to them. And the fact that she could listen to her son and Levi chatter all day long was telling. Her heart had opened a little bit more by the time the plane landed in Montana.

She just couldn't figure out why he didn't seem upset about the photos and the obvious manipulated lies.

CHAPTER SEVENTEEN

Jake had been right: the Montana ranch house was really nice and big, and a great place for them to stay when they traveled to the Montana ranch. There was a separate house for the foreman, who Jake had said had been running the ranch for a good while; his reputation was a good one and they kept him on. Gordon met them at the airstrip and drove them to the ranch house. Then he'd gone home to his wife, but would meet Levi the next morning to talk about the plans for the week. Gordon's wife had left them a meal warming in the warming tray in the kitchen.

After he and Rita had settled their suitcases into their rooms and Toby was running happily through the house, checking out the slipperiness of the hardwood floors and the wide stairs that led to the second floor, they took plates from the cabinet and set them out on the big island bar and got everything set up before they called Toby to eat.

It was a late lunch and they could eat the leftovers for supper. There was no way that he was having Rita cook; though she suggested she could cook while they were there, that wasn't her job. Even though she had told him that it was also not his job to have to look after her son the whole trip and she could do some cooking. He finally conceded that maybe if they got in early and she just really wanted to, but then Gordon's wife was prepared to do the cooking. She took care of the house and was supposed to take care of the cooking when they were visiting. It was a concept that was hard for Rita to grasp, it seemed. She wasn't used to having people cook for her. He wasn't either, but he had gotten used to it with Scotty at the ranch. It just came in handy sometimes.

Now, as they sat down to eat, Toby yawned. He had stayed awake the whole plane ride. He did take naps sometimes, but on the plane it was so exciting for him, he had talked the whole time and Levi had enjoyed talking with him. He thought Rita had enjoyed listening to the two of them because he really like teasing Toby and he enjoyed watching her smile, though she did seem distracted several times during the flight.

After they had eaten, she took her son to the room that she and Toby were sharing. She had wanted to keep him close because they were in a strange house he wouldn't be used to.

He went out to check on the barns. It was a great place. He liked Montana; he liked the wide-open spaces. He loved Texas but Jake had been right—he was excited about this place, about expanding here and about the possibilities. His phone rang while he was walking through the barn. It was Bret.

"Hey, what's up?"

Bret grunted on the other end of the line. "Nothing good."

His brother wasn't one to normally be down but he heard it in his voice. "Something wrong?"

"My shoulder's messed up. It's been giving me

problems. I rode bad again last night. Spent the day with the compresses on and ice packs. I don't know if I'm going to be ready for the next ride."

Bret had had a good run in bull riding. But he was well aware that there came a time when you had to give it up and all of them knew that time was approaching. But nobody could tell Bret to give it up until Bret was ready. "You going to ride?"

"I don't know. I'll just see. I've got 'til tomorrow night. So how's the ranch?"

"So far so good. We just got here and had lunch. I'm checking out the barn while Rita gets Toby down for a nap. We're going to tour tomorrow. I like Gordon—he seems like a good man."

"Good. I'll have to get out there and check it out. Jake's telling me—well, you know what Jake's telling us—he loved it."

Bret sounded really down. He lived a life of pretty much being on the road and Levi was too much of a homebody to want that. He never really even rodeoed; he liked being on the ranch. He liked the aspect of working cattle and growing oats and keeping the land up for the cattle so they'd be healthy and maintenance of the land. He had never been drawn to riding in a competition like that. Although he had ridden a couple of bulls in his day, it wasn't what drove him. But Bret loved it.

"I don't know, Bret. I'm looking around and there's a lot of space out here. You might have to come check it out—could be a good place to raise some bulls."

"You trying to get me out of Texas?"

"I'm just trying to get you to show some interest. You sound really down, brother."

"It will pass as soon as this shoulder feels better and I get to ride."

"You know, there is more to life than the ride."

"That's what y'all keep telling me, anyway."

He chuckled. At least this sounded more like Bret. "You should try it sometime."

"You know I love this lifestyle. I mean, I get tired of being on the road but I like the excitement of the ride...the adrenaline rush. It's just not something I'm sure I want to give up."

"Bret, you and I both know it's not something you can always choose to give up. It's something you have to give up at some point. Your body just can't handle all that abuse. You already have bad knees and your shoulder—I mean, there's only so much doctors can do to keep you healthy. You're going to be in a bad way in your older years."

It was true. Bret was good but riding bulls was terrible on you. Through the years, his brother had had torn tendons, and bruised and broken ribs, displaced shoulders…he couldn't even name the list. He went right back to it as soon as the doctor would let him. Heck, half the time even when he had bruised ribs, he was still riding—just taped them up and got back on. He wasn't doing his best but he tried anyway. Bull riders were tough—sometimes too tough for their own good.

"How about that Rita? Jake said you might be in love. I saw the tabloid of y'all kissing."

"We weren't kissing. And Jake should keep his mouth shut." Levi should have known Jake would open his mouth.

"That picture sure looked like it and Jake sure does believe it. I saw some pretty strong connection between you two when I was home the other night."

"So yeah, what the heck? Bret, some of us have to move forward with our lives, you know, and it's the truth. I might be in love. 'Course, I'm not going to tell you if I am or not but I figure I have to convince myself and Rita of the fact first." *Why couldn't he just come out and say he was in love?*

"If you two got married, you'd have an instant family. That'd make Mom happy. They were really getting on like buddies at dinner the other night."

"Yeah, they were." His mother had fallen for Toby, just like he had. And she'd loved talking with Rita.

"If that tabloid headline were true, Mom would be thrilled to have two of her sons finally married."

"Hey, I'm not married yet—don't be jumping the gun on me. I'll let you know when or if it happens."

Bret laughed and that made him smile.

"I thought I'd rile you up," Bret said.

"Well, at least you sound a little more perky now.

If it's at my expense, I guess I'm okay with that. You sure you're okay?"

"I'm fine. My dating life is in the pits. Not that I'm very good at it. I don't know what I'm looking for right now. My whole life just seems to be turning on its head a little bit, you know?"

"Yeah, I know. But hang in there. You'll feel better—you'll probably get out there tomorrow and do great on your ride. And some pretty lady will catch your eye and you'll be all happy again."

"You sound like I'm a guy who just jumps from one relationship to the next, just for a pretty face. That's not me, you know that."

"I know that." The truth was Bret had been hurt really bad once early by a local girl he'd hoped to marry. They'd all expected them to get married, but things fell apart and it hadn't happened. "Well, look, come on home whenever you feel like it. You know you always have that option."

"I know but I'm not ready to throw in the towel just yet. Anyway, I just wanted to call and say hey and see if you were ready to put on a tux and trade rings with this pretty lady. I'm glad for you, man. Really, I am, and just want to say if you think this woman is good for you, don't let her pass you up."

"Thanks. But like I said, I'll let you know."

After they hung up, he just stood there for a minute, thinking about what a weird conversation that had been. His brother must be thinking his life choices over really hard. Making a change in your life was not easy, especially when you loved something as much as Bret loved bull riding. Levi just hoped he got out before he got injured too badly.

As for him, he was just glad to be here and looking forward to spending time with Rita and Toby.

* * *

The Montana ranch was beautiful and she enjoyed their first two days there. She had met Gordon and Mary, his wife, who was cooking the meals. She was a lovely older woman. Her grandson was coming to stay a couple of days with them and she had asked whether maybe Toby would want to spend time with them on

Wednesday and Thursday while they were checking out the ranch.

Toby had ridden the helicopter with them the day before and that had been an experience for both of them. She had never been in a helicopter and it was a little nerve-racking. But Levi had told her that if the weather was the least bit dangerous, they wouldn't fly. And, true to his word, it had been a beautiful day. It was a rugged land they had flown over. They had seen the cattle and the ravines and just a wide expanse of ranch. It would take days to ride over this on horseback. He had explained that the Montana ranches were larger because there was less grass for the cattle, so it was a little different ranching.

She was glad that today they were going closer in the truck and though she had enjoyed the helicopter, she would need more time on the ground with the photos she was taking for him. She had some spectacular shots, though. The helicopter had landed several places, and they had gotten out and she'd taken photos of the rugged old windmills. But tonight, they were going to catch a few at sunset. She had thought it would be a great picture.

So now she smiled at Mary as she had driven the truck over to the foreman's house. "You're sure you don't mind?"

"Oh, I don't mind at all. I'm excited. Toby and Calvin are going to have a great time. Calvin's always saying when he comes, he never has anybody to play with and even though he's a year older than Toby, they'll have a great time."

"All right."

Toby was grinning. He was thrilled to get to play with the little boy. He hadn't seen anyone his size in a while. There was a big swing set they had at the back of their place just for when Calvin came to visit. So there was going to be lots of swinging, and she even had a little pool for them to play in that was about two feet of water. They were just going to have a day of splashing and fun.

"Then he's all yours." She bent down and held him by the shoulders. "Now you be a good boy. And you and Calvin have a great time, but you mind Miss Mary, okay?"

"I will, Mama. You take good pictures. And tell Mr. Levi I'll go with him on another day."

"I'll tell him." She smiled and then, after they had exchanged a few more bits of conversation, she got back in the truck and headed back to the barn, where Levi was going over some things with Gordon. She had spent the last two days trying to concentrate on her work, wanting to give Levi and his family the best shots that she could because she was so grateful for the help they were giving her. But she was excited that today, for the first time in a while, she and Levi were actually going to spend some time alone.

She was a little bit worried about that and about how much she was anticipating that time. He had been so good and though there were times where she would catch him looking at her and she thought he was, like her, thinking about how interested she was in him and hoping he might be interested in her, she laughed at the thought. It felt kind of adolescent, actually. But there was no denying it. Anyway, today it would be just the two of them. She had packed a lunch—leftover chicken from the night before, some cobbler that Mary had baked them, and a lot of water—and they were ready.

He smiled when she walked in the barn. "You ready? Toby good?"

"He's very happy and he told me to tell you that he'll go with you on another day. But I can tell you, Gordon, he's looking forward to spending time with Mary and Calvin. He hasn't played with another little boy in a while. Before I picked him up at my mother's, he didn't have anyone there to play with and since I've been here, it's just been the guys at the ranch. I'm very grateful they spend so much time with him, but there's nothing like playing with somebody your own size."

Gordon chuckled. "I know what you mean. Calvin's looking forward to it, too. When we told him that when he came to visit there would be another little boy here for him to play with, he could hardly contain his excitement. And Mary, she loves it. She would love to have more grandchildren but I'm not sure she's ever going to get them. So this is great and she's really good with kids, so you just go on. You have a good day and don't worry about him. And if y'all get in late, we'll just lay him down with Calvin. Okay?"

"Thanks, Gordon. We really appreciate everything

you're doing. We're really glad to have you here. You and Mary."

"Hey, I'm just glad someone who views the land and loves it like I do when I bought this place. I've been here a long time. The previous owners loved this ranch and they had a fear that when they had to put it up for sale—you know, he just got too old to handle it and his kids just didn't want to be stuck to the land like he was—he was afraid it was going to get broken up into small parcels. So he and I were both thrilled to have y'all buy the whole ranch. So, anyway, y'all go have a good time."

Levi shook his hand and then they all headed out of the barn. He opened the door for her and she climbed in, and then he went around and got in. "All right, I guess we're off."

She smiled and chuckled. He looked so excited. "I think you're as excited about exploring as Toby was about playing with Calvin today."

Levi drove the truck toward the ranch road they were taking and shot a grin at her. "I'm excited. But I have to tell you, Rita Snow, I'm excited about spending a little time alone with you today. I know I'm not supposed to say that, but it's true. I'll behave but I think you'll be able to relax a little more today. Toby is a great kid and I enjoy him, but I know that taking pictures and watching him at the same time and worrying about me having to watch him, it kind of stresses you out just a little bit."

"It does a little bit but it's been great, so here we go. This will be an adventure."

"I hope so."

CHAPTER EIGHTEEN

The ranch was expansive. During the ride in the helicopter, they had seen so many variations of terrain, and it was impressive. They were driving toward some canyons that they'd seen and wanted to explore a little bit. She could only imagine the pictures she could get, although she had gotten some great shots from the air. She itched to be on the ground and close up to the beauty that she had seen. It took over an hour to drive to the section they were heading to.

But she didn't mind; she enjoyed every moment spent with Levi. They laughed as he told jokes; he was funny. She told him some funny stories about Toby growing up. He was a funny little boy, and Levi was very good about asking about Toby. He had never had children and he was single, but he seemed genuinely interested in her son. She told him about the time that Toby had terrified her when he had gotten away from her in Walmart when he was a toddler. She had just set him down to stand and was pushing the cart back into the cart corral; she had just turned her back on him for a second and when she turned around, he was gone.

"I was horrified. You know, I couldn't breathe—my heart was about to pound out of my chest. It was the scariest moment of my entire life. I raced through the store, calling his name. I couldn't leave the front area but I kept it in sight and just went all around right in there, hollering for him. Everyone looked at me in horror that I would have lost my child like that. But they were so kind and the store managers locked the front door so that just in case someone had tried to take him they couldn't get out. My fear was that he was already gone because I was at the buggy area near the registers, and I thought maybe I'd set him down and someone had snatched him up and just raced through the door.

"And Toby—you know Toby…he's just the

friendliest little baby. He probably wouldn't have even screamed. He probably would have just wrapped his arms around whoever it was and given them a big kiss as they carried him away from me. And then, about the time I was about to pass out—and I'm sure less than five minutes had passed of me being so horror filled, the managers all jumping in to help me—he jumped out from beneath a rack of pants. The women's clothing section was just right there. It was a small Walmart—it wasn't a great big gigantic store. It was one of the smaller ones and everything's closer together. He jumped out and yelled 'boo.' I just fell to my knees right there in front of everyone, held open my arms, and just squalled. I was mad and angry and scared and upset and all I could do was kiss him and kiss him and hold him and cry.

"Everyone clapped and Toby—he was clueless. He looked around and he just grinned, thinking everybody was clapping for him. They were, but he thought he had done something good. He had no idea he had just about given his mother a heart attack and scared the poor manager and all the people working there and the guests that were there, too—the shoppers. Needless to say, I aged a little bit that day. I probably have gray hair because of that day. I learned my lesson big-time—I never turn my back on Toby. Never. At least, not in the store. He gets a little freedom around the house and here since we've been on your ranch, but before that, I was super protective. Partly because of him—he just loves to play hide-and-seek and he loves to hide, and I just never know…he could hide and something terrible could happen."

How had their fun conversation shifted to something that had her heart failing with the terror she had felt gripping her throat right then and there? Levi slowed as he kept one hand on the steering wheel, while he reached over, cupped her cheek. The distance in his truck wasn't too far away for him to be able to reach her like that. She could not move; she just stared at him.

He smiled, glanced to make sure he was still driving the truck straight, then looked back at her. "You are a good mother, and that little boy is sweet and good and good-natured because he's like you. And no, he didn't mean to hurt you or scare you, but I know he did and I'm so sorry. Don't let it get you down right now. Calm down. It's all okay."

She did calm down. The instant panic attack she had begun to have just thinking about losing Toby eased away and in its place, she just looked at the beautiful, wonderful, handsome man who was her boss. "Thank you, Levi. I just still get upset when I think about it. And thank you for the kind words. If I'm half as sweet and nice as Toby, then, gee, I must be wonderful."

She laughed and Levi looked back at her from where he had glanced at the pasture again. His thumb traced along her cheek to her jaw and then back up to her cheek and back down to her jaw. The gentle, soothing caress sent pulsing vibrations through her entire body, electrifying every nerve ending in her. She had never known such a touch.

"I think, I'm hoping, that when you get your shop open in Fredericksburg and I'm not your boss anymore, that you would go out with me?"

The earnest look in his eyes captured her heart.

Here he was asking her, telling her he was attracted to her and wanted to go out with her but because of her experience she had had with her previous bosses, he wasn't about to make any kind of move on her until after he was not her boss anymore. Just the very idea of that blew her away.

"That would be wonderful. I don't classify you in the same category as I classify my previous bosses. You need to know that, Levi. You've been nothing but good to me."

She placed her hand over his, pulled it down, and held it with both her hands. He pressed the brake and pulled the truck to a halt. The land around them was rugged and barren, and not the most beautiful spot in the world. They were headed to a beautiful spot; here it was fairly bleak but the feel of his hand in hers and the look in his eyes made it alive with color. She saw nothing but beauty surrounding them.

When he put the truck in park and then leaned toward her, he took her hand in his. He lifted it to his lips and kissed her palm. "I really care for you. I just want you to know that. And I would never do anything to hurt you."

She couldn't help herself, feeling bolder than she had ever felt, because she had never wanted anything more strongly than she wanted a kiss from Levi in that moment. She moved across the bench seat of the ranch truck and into the circle of his arms, and she kissed him. He looked startled; she saw his eyes as she moved in for the kiss. And then he sighed as their lips met; his arms went around her and he kissed her back. Sitting there in the middle of nowhere, she had never experienced anything remotely like the powerful kiss that Levi was giving her. His arms crushed her to him, and his lips were very intent on making sure that she knew that he cared for her. She smiled, even as their lips kissed.

He must have felt the movement of her lips moving upward. He pulled back and his eyes were dancing as he smiled at her. "Is that funny?"

She let out a breath. "Oh no, there's nothing funny about that kiss at all. I'm just overwhelmed. I've never felt anything like that. I couldn't help but smile. That tabloid photographer would have really gotten a shot if he'd snapped that kiss." She hadn't meant to blurt that out. She'd tried not to say anything all week, thinking he just didn't want to mention it and she hadn't known how to mention it. But this kiss had tilted her world and the words just came out.

He raked a hand through his hair. Somewhere along the kiss, his hat had fallen off and lay halfway between the steering wheel and floorboard.

"I'm going to agree with you on that. Wow. Okay, so I'm going to say for both our sakes that you go back over there in your seat and I'll scoot right here into my seat, and I'll hold onto the steering wheel with both hands and you hang on to the door handle over there with both hands, and let's see if we can drive the rest of the way to the canyon and let these feelings calm down a little bit. And I didn't mention the tabloid because I didn't want to make you feel weird."

She smiled. "I understand. And maybe you're right about keeping those hands on the wheel and your foot on the gas pedal." Smiling, she did as he asked; she moved over to the passenger seat.

He winked at her, then pressed the gas pedal and they started driving toward their destination once more.

But all she could think about as he drove was that before the day was over, he was going to have to let go of that steering wheel and she was going to be ready. And there was no one around to take a picture of them.

CHAPTER NINETEEN

The rest of the way, Levi lambasted himself. *What had he been thinking?* Of course, now that he had kissed her, all he was thinking about was kissing her again. And again and again and again and for the rest of his life. Yup, he was a goner. But he couldn't scare her off. They hadn't known each other long enough and he just had to get a grip.

He had to get control of himself right now. He didn't want to cross any kind of lines that were between boss and employee. He never wanted to be classified with the other jerks who had been in her life. So, as he drove, he talked to himself—told himself to get a grip and to take this relationship back a notch…or two or three. He just needed to rewind. And he knew that was going to be hard. But in the end, she was worth it.

When they reached the canyon, he drove along the ridge at a safe distance and found an overlook that had an amazing view. He stopped the truck and had to talk himself into letting go of the steering wheel. He glanced over at her.

She was smiling at him. "It's okay, Levi. I'm not going to attack you. So please, you can relax."

"And I'm not going to attack you either. But we're going to have to control that right there."

After they got out of truck, she said, "Okay. Stand right there. Come on, I know you don't want to be in this picture but it's your property—you need to be in this picture, cowboy." Rita grinned at Levi.

She had him stand where she could get a picture of the canyon behind him. He was frowning at her right now, teasing her because she had talked him into letting her get some shots of him on the property. She had taken several shots of the canyon and happened to get one of him in the picture and decided she needed more.

"Okay, okay. Take your shots." He grinned and laughed when she made a face at him and then began snapping photos. Teasing her, he cocked a hip and put a hand on his thigh, dipped his chin and gave her a come-hither look from beneath the brim of his Stetson.

She laughed and snapped the photo.

He held his hands up. "Okay, that one's not for real. We have to delete that one."

"If you say so. But I think it's really cute."

"Well, I was just joking, getting in on your fun time there. I'm not really into looking cute."

She set her camera down across her chest, let it hang from the strap around her neck, and put her hands on her hips and squinted at him through the sunshine. "Well, I hate to give you the news, Levi, but you are cute. Handsome. You could be a male model—a cowboy model. I hear that they are desperate for cowboy models for all these romance books that are being written and published. You'd make a good one. Why don't you do a few poses? We could get several shots and then I might upload them, and I could make a lot of money."

He shook his head and grinned. "I don't think so. I'm not sure I can handle being on the cover of a romance novel any better than I handle being on the cover of a tabloid."

"You're missing your calling."

He laughed and walked forward. "Come on. I think it's time to eat before we get delirious. I think you might be hungry or thirsty or something."

She turned and fell into step beside him. They had set a blanket out on the ground as they roamed and now he went to the truck and grabbed an ice chest and carried it over. Out here in this heat, a picnic basket wouldn't do; they had to have an ice chest that would keep everything cool.

He opened it up and began to pull out the food they had packed. Once they had the sandwiches and the pitcher of ice tea and the chocolate brownies that she had baked set out on the blanket, she sat down cross-legged and handed him a napkin. He sat down on the edge and left his boots hanging off the side of the blanket; he crossed his ankles, leaned back on one arm, thanked her for the napkin, and then reached back for a sandwich. She had made some chicken salad from the left-over chicken that the housekeeper had prepared for them. She had also found, among the bread that Mary had stocked the pantry with, some very soft, beautiful croissants so she had made the chicken salad sandwiches on the croissants. The delicate texture of the croissant and the tanginess of the chicken salad just went so well together.

"This looks really good. Kind of girly."

She shook her head at him. "You won't care how it looks once you taste it. I agree it's not quite like those Texas dips made with that thick, tough, hoagie bread and slices of prime rib for you to dip into that steak broth, but I bet you're going to love it."

He took a bite, grinned while keeping his mouth closed, which made his mouth turn up at the edges, and his eyes widened. He nodded as he chewed. When he could speak, he gave her a thumbs-up. "I have to agree—that was good. Might have to start ordering that when I go to the diner. I've seen it on there."

"It's very popular. The two just go so well together. Now that the kidding's all aside, this place is amazing. So y'all are going to just start a new cattle business out here?"

"That's the plan. We'll have to hire more staff and, to be honest, there's a lot we can do out here. We're closer to the wild mustangs. We figure we can start a bigger rescue mission out here with our mustangs and a fostering program. The thought of the mustangs being in so much trouble just doesn't sit right with us. And, well, like we're fond of saying, we hit all that oil for some reason—it certainly wasn't to make us happier cowboys or for us to change our ways or what we're like. But we look at it as an opportunity to expand our business while helping good causes we believe in. And that's one of them. So having a ranch out here puts us in a different area for something like that. Plus, raising cattle's a good thing out here. So that's why we bought it.

"We're going to offer the main foreman job to the foreman they've got right now, but he's let us know that as the operation increases, he's not going to want to take on the whole job. So we're going to hopefully hire from our guys back home who know how we like to do business and move some of them out here if they want to. Probably some of our single guys—we're not sure if we have any married foreman material who would want to move out here. But we've heard from several of our single guys this might be a good place for them, so it's a good option anyway.

"There's some excitement building among the guys. Some of them have even talked about rotating in and out, maybe on a six-month basis. We'll have to see…it's a little different in the winter than Texas. One thing we can't complain about in Texas is our winters. But out here it gets cold—it gets dangerous and the guys will have to know what they're doing. It's good Gordon is going to stay on to at least help us through that, and then they'll maintain the house for us and the land around the area and just be there for consulting. There is a possibility that one of my brothers will come out here, maybe Bret if he ever comes to terms with what he's going to do with his life after the PBR and NFR. If not him, then who knows—it could be Jake. But Jake's really happy where he is, so I don't know. We've just got a lot of things on our minds right now.

Us coming out here and getting all these pictures is a good idea."

She felt relief at that because it was such a good thing to her, knowing she could be of such a help to them. Spending time with Levi was just an added bonus.

"I'm glad. This is beautiful land but I can see where it could be harsher, more remote—especially in the winter—than Texas. Me, I'm a Texas gal. If I were to ever re-marry, I'd have to tell my future husband that I don't want to move past the Texas border. I'm very partial to Texas."

His eyes twinkled and he hitched his lip up on one side as he considered her. "Well then, darlin', I don't want to jump the gun or anything, but that means I could be in the running because I, too, love Texas and I don't ever plan on leaving the Hill Country border, much less the Texas border. And I'll just let you know that right now."

His words settled in her heart, and she knew he wasn't talking idly. He was feeling the same unnerving connection to her that she was feeling toward him. But she could not mix this up too much. "Levi, you know we really need to think about this. There is something between us and that is undeniable, and you're telegraphing it to me pretty bluntly. I'm praying you're not just pulling my leg on that."

"I'm not."

"That's kind of what I thought, but there's a lot at stake here. For one, I've got to get my business up and going. I've got to be able to stand on my own. And I think we need to know, that for me, that I could stand on my own—I never want anybody to say I married you because I had to because I needed support. I'm just too independent for that. And right now, I need you. I need you for what you're helping me do in the desperate situation I felt like I was in with my mother-in-law, trying to steadily inch her way into getting Toby from me. I don't want to mess up the fact that what you're doing for me is going to enable me to get my business started. I really need time to get all that worked out."

He set his sandwich down, leaned over toward her, and placed his palm against the side of her face, cupping her face so gently as his eyes dug into hers with sincere understanding. "I totally get where you're coming from. So that's just like what we talked about—we're going to give this time. We're not going to rush anything. I just need you to know that I'm the kind of guy who doesn't just jump into things. Not anymore. When I was young and stupid and idiotic right after we got all that money, it did change me for a while, and the tabloids picked up on it. They did not paint a pretty picture about me, so I work really hard to counteract all that these days. I want this to go slow and steady, and when you're on your feet, then we can get this figured out. I just need you to know I'm in this. I'm in this all the way, and I promise I would never hurt you. And part of that includes trying to keep those tabloids off you as much as I can. Okay?"

She loved him. She knew it was true and undeniable. Her heart thundered. "Okay. Thank you. Nice and slow."

CHAPTER TWENTY

Two weeks after they got home from Montana, Levi helped Rita move out of the cabin. It was one of the hardest things he had ever done. But he was determined that he was going to give her the shot at starting up her business like she needed to. They had been able to keep themselves out of the limelight over the course of the last two weeks. There had been a few kisses—which he had been very grateful for—and there had been some sitting on the porch swing together and some cuddling that made his day. But they did all that away from the eyes of everybody. He was determined that nobody was going to leak anything about them to anybody. And if any of his guys suspected there was something going on between them, they had not leaked it to anybody. Which was a good thing because he had already told his guys, warned them that if anything on his property got leaked, he'd know it was one of them and he would find out who it was and they'd be fired on the spot. When it came to those tabloids, he was hardcore. And when it came to Rita and Toby, it was even worse than that.

Now he and his guys loaded up the washed-out cattle trailer with a few things that she had. They carried the furnishings from the cabin upstairs. He had insisted that until she found what she needed that she was going to borrow the things out of the cabin so she would have a couch and a chair and a bed and that when she found just what she wanted, then they'd come pick it up. But right now, it was on loan. It was better than just handing her the money and telling her to go buy whatever she wanted—which he could have done, but she wouldn't have taken it. She was a practical woman; he knew she wasn't going to have Toby sleeping on an air mattress if she could help it, so she had accepted his offer.

Now, as far as downstairs went, she had been saving her money for her business and she was going to purchase a few things. The last two weeks, she'd taken some time to find some flea markets. They were pretty much done with their photos and the editing process, so she had several hours a day to borrow his truck and explore. She had headed off to Round Top one day when they were having their big, gigantic sale. The flea market attracted thousands of people and spread over miles. She came back with several items that she'd gotten as great buys and he was eager to see what she could do in there. He wasn't charging her any rent for the first several months. He wanted to do a year, but she had flat out refused, so he had given her the three months she insisted on. He knew if she wasn't making a profit in three months, she was going to be terribly disappointed in herself. So he was praying hard that her business would take off.

To their credit, Cole and Tulip had loved the shots of their wedding she had taken and insisted that she use them on the walls to display her work so that she would have the start of a portfolio there at Hill

Country. Plus, they knew that their wedding had been *the* wedding in the Hill Country and that it would give her some buzz. And, thankfully, with the website she had set up, some calls had come in. She was excited and that excited him.

He wanted very much for her to succeed. He wanted very much to marry her. He loved her desperately. And he prayed that nothing happened between now and whenever she would decide that she loved him like that too. There was a flame of concern that rode low in his gut and boiled like hot lava. And that would be there until she said yes, she would marry him. He just prayed it was soon, or he was going to have a hole through his gut and his soul. One he didn't think he would ever get over.

He and Jake, who had volunteered to help them, and the two cowboys they had roped into also helping, walked up the stairs. Jake walked backward carefully so he didn't trip as he helped carry the overstuffed leather recliner up to the apartment.

Rita stood at the top of the landing, holding Toby's hand and smiling. "You two are doing great.

Just don't trip, Jake. Don't run him over, Levi. I'd hate to have to call the ambulance when you fall down those steep stairs."

"Yeah, tell him to slow down, would ya." Jake laughed.

While she was talking, her phone rang. "Okay, guys, excuse me. I'm going to go take this. But just keep being careful—you just got a little ways to go."

Jake looked at him. "So I know you're trying to keep this on the down-low but, dude, I'm watching you from right here, and you are crazy about that woman. I can see it on your face. All she has to do is smile at you or even say something, and you light up like a lighthouse."

Levi couldn't lie to his brother; he gave him a warning. "Keep that to yourself. I'm going to marry that woman if she'll have me, but I just have to wait until she has this business going. So you do me a favor—you have anybody who's getting married, you send their business her way."

Jake laughed. "You got it, brother. I can't wait to see you marry. That will be the day. Just don't try to throw any garters at me when you get married. Like Cole slapping you in the chest at his wedding. See there—you have fallen in love—it's like the garter thing works."

He laughed. It was the first time he actually thought about it. "You know, you might be right. He threw that at me, and it's like I fell for Rita hard and fast. So, hey, if I can get her to marry me—got to get over that hurdle first—I might be aiming my garter that I throw at you. Might be fun to see if the thing Cole's been talking about really works. That if you get hit with that garter or you catch that garter, next person you see is the one you fall in love with 'cause it happened to him and Tulip."

They reached the top of the landing. Jake stopped, making Levi halt. "If you want me to send business this way to help you in your quest, then I wouldn't be threatening me with things like that. I am not ready to get married. I'm going to be the holdout. I'm the baby boy. No reason for me to get married, yet you guys are wanting to do it all for us."

"I guess we'll just have to wait and see who comes up next."

Jake laughed and backed up onto the landing, and then they turned and went inside.

Rita was at the bar area of the little apartment, scribbling on a piece of paper. She looked up at him and smiled, beaming. She was gorgeous.

They moved on inside and set the chair down, and she ended the call. And, then to his surprise, she raced over and threw her arms around him. He saw Jake's eyes widen and then he gave him a grin over her shoulder.

His arms automatically went around her as she exclaimed, "I have my first customer! Someone saw the photos online and it's a big wedding. It's someone who knows y'all and it starts soon. Their photographer had to bow out. They were scrambling to find somebody so they're going to use me. I'm going to go meet with them and do some preliminary scheduling. But thank you. This is going to be so exciting."

He just held onto her as long as she would let him. "Yes, it is, and you deserve it. Your photos are awesome. And because you have such a big heart and a good heart, that's going to shine through. I told you that you were going to be a success."

She looked at him, tears in her eyes. "You did, and I have to tell you, Levi, nobody has ever had my back. And I just need to thank you for that."

Jake stepped in. "Hey, Rita, I think it'd be safe to say that as of now, we all have your back. Especially Levi—not that I'm going to tell anybody. But the Tanners—we've got your back—don't you worry about that. And like Levi said, this is going to be a success. I saw your work, too. I don't know much about pictures but, man, you made my brother look good in those pictures."

They all laughed at that.

Toby ran over and threw his arms around Levi and his mama, and looked up at them. "I'm happy too."

Levi had to agree.

CHAPTER TWENTY-ONE

Rita was thrilled with her first job. She had very nearly started crying the day that she had gotten the call and had thrown herself at Levi in her excitement, not even caring that Jake was standing there. She had just been so happy and because she was in love with Levi, it was a natural reaction to share her excitement with him. So she had just thrown herself at him and of course his arms had opened wide, and he had welcomed her unquestionably.

Of course, she was a little concerned when Toby had thrown his arms around their legs and told them he was happy. She had to remember that in all of this, Toby was the one who could get hurt the worst if something did not come of her and Levi's budding relationship. She had been through so much in her life. Dan had run around on her and the night he'd died in that car wreck, he'd shoved her off the steps leading into the garage and she'd fallen hard. He had been so mad that she'd confronted him that he hadn't even checked on her. He'd just gotten into his car and driven off, leaving her there, nine months pregnant. She'd gone into labor while he raced off. She'd managed to crawl up the steps and make it to a phone to call for an ambulance to take her to the hospital. That night, she'd had Toby and lost Dan. He'd died in the emergency room while she was in the delivery room, having his son. He'd shredded her trust but left her with the biggest blessing of her life, Toby.

And she would never let anyone take Toby or harm him.

But she trusted Levi, and that was just the truth of it. She trusted Levi and he had told her he would never hurt her. But she had to get her life in order, if she were to ever have a life with him. And this wedding was her ticket to that.

Tulip dropped by, the tiny bell tingling as she walked into the shop.

Toby was coloring and immediately jumped up and raced over and hugged Tulip.

"Having fun today, buddy?"

"I'm coloring. Want to color with me?"

"Let me talk to your mom for a minute, then I sure will color with you."

Satisfied with that, Toby went back to his play area and started coloring again. She'd fixed his area up with toys to keep him busy, which came in handy considering business was picking up. She owed a lot of it to Tulip and Cole, who had graciously given her the go-ahead to use their name and display her photos of them. That had given her a lot of exposure.

"So what are you up to today?" she asked as Tulip sat down in the barstool next to the counter. She looked beautiful and happy in her sundress and her hair pulled back with a couple of tendrils falling from the sides, holding the rest of it back in a small clasp.

"I am just coming by to check this place out. I hear all kinds of good stuff. You are hot."

Rita laughed, feeling just so happy. "And part of that is because of you. Thank you so much for all the good PR you are giving me. You and Cole. It's like y'all are my own cheering section. And this is a great area—so many weddings. And with the company we hired to help me with my website getting top listing on the SEO and search engines, it's just helping me so much."

"We were so happy to do it. And, to be honest, we all know there is something between you and Levi. I know y'all aren't talking about it." She leaned forward so that Toby didn't hear. "Just so you know, I know, and realize it's a little secret between y'all, but we are excited about you two. Cole is just beside himself. He was hoping that some of his brothers would start thinking about settling down, because we are very happy. Very happy, may I repeat. And his mother and daddy—oh my goodness, I was on the phone with them yesterday and they were just raving about the possibilities. They've been excited since they met you. That day at dinner, they could already tell that he was crazy about you. We all could."

What did she say to that? "You see too much." She chuckled.

"Y'all's feelings for each other are on display, and you just think nobody sees it. But we're just very thrilled and ready for y'all to come clean."

"My lips are sealed. I was just about to take Toby to lunch. You want to go to lunch?"

"I want to go to lunch, and I think we need to go checking out some stores. You need more furniture in here. Forward the calls to your cell phone. I'm doing a design intervention here. You need comfy chairs for consultations. A table over there, with maybe some picture books you can thumb through. Because you can't put all the pictures on your wall. You know you're going to have some, so we can just anticipate. There's a new store down the street. I don't go shopping a lot, but I just happened to go in there the other day and they've got some really cute upholstered chairs."

"Well, I don't want to spend too much but, sure, that'd be fun."

Tulip stood and after she got Toby, they locked up the shop and walked down the street. Fredericksburg was alive with tourists right now; wine country was open and lots of people came for the weekend. It was a great time to have opened up. A lot of the weddings were already booked but she was getting some calls about fall weddings. And this one that was going to help pay for her opening just happened to be a fill-in job, which was a blessing straight from heaven.

It was exactly what she needed, because it was going to fund her opening and help her pay Levi back on their three-month deadline and be officially supporting herself and Toby. He hadn't mentioned it again but Levi wanted her to that point, also. She knew he had a wedding on his own mind and she did too. She just had to stand on her own two feet first.

They went to lunch in the courtyard of one of the restaurants in the center of town and ordered ice teas as they talked. She really was crazy about Tulip. And thankful that she had somebody, a woman, to confide in if she needed to.

"So how's the in-law situation?" She had chosen her words carefully, knowing Toby had no idea what in-law meant.

She had told Tulip about her mother-in-law

hoping to find a weakness in her ability to support Toby and try to gain custody of him. "She knows her dream isn't going to happen. I can prove I can support us now. I've explained she can see you-know-who, whenever she wants to. She seems ready to come here for a visit. You know, grief can make a person change for the good or the bad. But love can heal a broken heart and, in this case, I'm going to do all I can to help her heal. Just not give up what belongs with me." As in Toby.

Tulip patted her arm. "I hear you. All the more reason or the main reason, I guess I should say, for us to get you more business and make sure you're set up good."

"Thank you. I cannot even imagine you doing any more for me than you already are."

"Well, all I can say is if I see an opportunity, I'm going to chat people up about you. And who knows? You may get another wedding out of it real quick. We'll just have to say our prayers that that really happens. If you had another big gig, then I think you'll pretty much be set. Because your work's going to get recommendations just because it's so great."

"Thank you for your vote of confidence." *If only it were all true.*

* * *

The next few weeks passed quickly for Rita. Her first wedding went off without a hitch. She'd made friend's with Arlene who owned the icecream shop a few doors down from her shop and she had a little boy Toby's age and she'd watched Toby for her. Then, maybe it was beginner's luck but whatever it was, she took it and ran because everything went perfectly. The guests were thrilled with the wedding, and she had had several consults with friends of the bride and of the groom, who were of that age where they were engaged and planning weddings. Some of them had already engaged photographers but had still come to consult with her just in case they also had an emergency and lost their photographer, they would have Rita on standby. But two of the young ladies had booked events and she had had one just last weekend; it had been quick and she had had to scramble to get it done, just like she had had to scramble to get the other one done. But the next one, she had several months to get ready for and now she was having a little bit of a breather. Laura had come to pick up Toby and had taken him back to Amarillo for a visit.

Now Rita was missing him so much and again worried that Laura would hound her about trying to get him to live with her full-time. This time, her mother-in-law had said that she realized with her busy schedule she wouldn't have time to give enough attention to her grandson. She had actually called him "her grandson" instead of by his name. It was just to get her point across that she had rights, too; she was his grandmother.

Levi had been staying in the picture and true to his word, he hadn't tried to carry their relationship any further. It was as if now that she had her own business and, at this point, was able to even pay him the small rental fee that she had insisted that he at least charge her, he had withdrawn. And she was beginning to worry about that because she didn't want him to withdraw. She had wanted him to want to date her. She wanted him to have feelings for her.

Tulip knew this. Tulip had picked up on it and though they talked, Tulip had a loyalty to Levi and his family and was trying not to overstep. But she said that Levi was just giving her time, that Cole had asked him about her and that he had said he was giving her time.

What did that mean exactly? Time to go crazy?

As she sat inside her office, her phone rang. One of the brides she had been talking to lately called to confirm that she did indeed want to give Rita a retainer and hire her to do her wedding. Relief flooded over Rita. She was really doing this. She was really on her way. But she didn't want to do it without Levi coming along for the ride with her and Toby. *So what did she do? Should she go after him and tell him her feelings? Or just wait?*

There was a tap on her front window. She looked up. As if she had wished him to be there, Levi stood at the door. Jumping up, she almost knocked over her glass of tea. She smoothed her skirt and then hurried from the desk through the studio to the door. She undid the deadbolt. Her heart rammed against her ribs; she knew, just from the feel of it, she had a goofy smile on her face.

He smiled back at her, those beautiful eyes of his twinkling.

"Levi, I'm so glad you're here. Come in."

"I couldn't stay away any longer. I came to ask you if you wanted to go out? Tulip told me that your mother-in-law had come and demanded that Toby go back to Amarillo with her for a visit. And I was worried about you. Worried that you were alone and sad, and I just couldn't do it anymore—I couldn't stay away. I had to come and check on you."

He had come to check on her. Whew, she loved this man. "Thank you. Levi, I've missed you. And I was sitting here, sad and worried about Toby being gone and worried that my mother-in-law was going to try to keep him. But I was thinking of you, too, and wondering why you hadn't been by these last few weeks. You just disappeared."

He closed the door behind him. "I didn't mean to disappear. I just meant to give you time. I want to court you. I want to give you time for us not to be, you know, boss and employee. I wanted to give you time to settle into your new business and get on your feet so you can feel like you were self-supporting and, you know, strong, like you said."

She smiled at him. That was Levi. Giving her time to adjust.

"That's all well and good, Levi, but you see the problem is I don't need time for any of that. I think you and I moved past that. I need you… I need you to be my friend." *She couldn't just come out and tell him she needed him to ask her to marry him—how would that look?*

The light in his eyes flickered and dimmed. "I see. Well then, you've got that. I guess a friend can still go out and eat with a friend, right?"

She smiled, unable to help herself. "Yes. And I'm starving. You are going to take me out now, right?"

He laughed.

Was it her imagination, or did the smile not quite meet his eyes?

"That's what I'm here for. I'm hungry too. You pick the restaurant and we'll either walk or drive."

She didn't care what she looked like. She didn't go check herself in the mirror; she just reached for her key ring hanging on a hook behind the lantern she had hanging right there at the doorway, and she slipped it around her wrist. "I'm starving. Let's hit the taco place."

"Tacos it is. You are not hard to please."

"Oh, don't say that." She pulled the door closed behind her, inserting the key and locking it. "Those tacos are amazing. I'm very hard to please but I'm just feeling like tacos, and I know the exact place I want to go."

"I do too. And I agree with your decision. But it's not a very expensive meal."

"And I know you can afford it but that's what I want. I'm an easy girl to please, isn't that what you said? I'm a cheap date."

They both laughed. Reaching down, he slipped his hand around hers. He looked at her, as if giving her a moment to take her hand from his.

She was not about to do that; instead, she intertwined her fingers with his and squeezed and smiled at him. "Although you might order me some queso, if that's not too much trouble."

"I'll even order you some chips to go with the queso. And a sweet tea. And dessert afterward, if you want it."

"Oh, I do. I'm a dessert kind of girl. Anything that prolongs eating it with you." She was being sappy but she couldn't help it. When Levi was around, she just felt that way. And it had been awhile, so she felt very sappy.

They strolled down the street, toward the courthouse along the main strip. When they got to the Mexican restaurant, he held the door and she walked in. They were seated quickly in a back booth. He still requested back booths. She noted that.

"So how have you been?" She wanted to hear everything about what he'd been doing on the ranch and how the cattle sale had gone. She hadn't gone to it because it happened to be the same weekend that she had her wedding, so that had meant that he was at the big sale and she was at the big wedding.

"It went great. Your photos were a huge hit. We made a lot of money and were able to donate a big chunk to charity for a good cause, and you were a big part of that. My brothers had all said to thank you."

Tulip had told her the same thing but she just wanted to hear Levi talk about what he had been doing. "I was glad to do it. Levi, after what y'all have done for me—what you've done for me—all you have to do is ask and I'll take pictures for you."

"Well, that's a relief because you're the only photographer I'd want to hire."

"Oh, you wouldn't have to pay me. You've done so much for me already."

"Aw, now don't go discounting your services. I'll always pay you—you're worth your time and you're excellent. Why wouldn't I pay you?"

"Because I'm trying to give you a gift."

"I don't need a gift. All I need..." He reached across the table and slipped his hand over hers, where she had it cupped next to her tea glass. He squeezed. His eyes held hers. "All I need is for you to be in my life."

Her breath caught. "And I'd like that. Because I'm kind of used to you, too, now."

"Well, good then. We're settled on that."

They were settled on it, only she wasn't exactly

sure what they had settled on. Was she in his life as a friend, as a girlfriend—maybe permanently? She needed to ask. But as the waitress walked up, Levi slipped his hand from hers and then instructed her to give her order. And she did, all the while worrying about what he had meant.

* * *

Levi had said exactly what he had wanted to say. She hadn't made it clear how much she wanted him in her life, and he wasn't sure he had made it clear that he wanted her as his wife. As they ate their meal, they talked about small stuff and her upcoming weddings that she had and how happy Toby was living here. They just never clarified what their status was. He was worried, though, about her mother-in-law. Worried she was going to try to take Toby from her. And that was another reason why he'd come today; he needed to talk to her about that. He needed to assure her that he had already spoken with Harold, and his law firm was ready to be behind her one hundred percent. Matter of fact, Harold had already drafted up a document for her mother-in-law on what her rights as a grandparent were by law, if she needed him to go as far as notify her that she would not be able to take Toby from her. But he couldn't do that without talking to Rita first.

When dinner was over and they had eaten their cheesecake, they left the restaurant and strolled down the street. Music could be heard coming from the various restaurants and bars along the way and it was a very pleasant evening. Romantic. And all he wanted to do was take her in his arms and kiss her, tell her how much he loved her. Because he did; he was still head over heels for her. But he had to get this out. "So I need to tell you, just to let you know that Harold's drafted up a document for you that tells your mother-in-law exactly what her rights are as a grandparent and what your rights are. It's just to let her know that you're not alone in this and if she tries to take Toby from you, you've got some power in this issue. And she'll have to fight to take Toby from you because there's no way I'm going to let that happen. We'll fight it all the way. I just need you to know that."

She stopped walking, just closed her eyes and stood there. After a minute, she opened those amazing eyes. "Levi, that's got to be the most heart-wrenching offer anyone's ever made to me. That you're willing to fight for my child—no one's ever given me a gift like that. And I can't thank you enough. But she is Toby's grandmother. And I just feel like if I were to do something like that, then our relationship might never recover. She's come around and knows she's not going to get him away from me. And I think she's okay with it. She was just sad and grieving."

"I'm sorry. I didn't mean to step over my boundaries or our friendship."

"You didn't—you were just trying to help me. I'm totally on board with that. I'm completely grateful to you. I've never had anybody support me like that. Knowing that your family and you are behind me is just a gift. Knowing that you are standing here with me right now is the greatest gift of all."

She stared at him for a long moment and his heart just cracked wide open. He wanted to hold her so bad. He needed to get over trying to be her hero and let her know he just wanted to be the man in her life who would love her forever. But her eyes darkened and she looked away. Uncertainty grabbed him by the throat and strangled him, and words wouldn't come.

"Levi," she looked back at him, uncertainty in her expression, "I'm kind of confused about where we stand right now. You said you wanted to be my friend."

"Yes, but—"

"But what about not just being friends but being more?" She licked her lips.

His heart pounded against his ribcage. "Are you saying you want to be more?"

She scowled. "Levi, do I have to spell it out? I love you. And I want you in my life. I want us."

His heart burst with happiness and a grin sprang to his lips. "That is the biggest relief—the most beautiful words I have heard. I love you." He cupped her face in his, standing right there on the sidewalk of Fredericksburg. "I love you, Rita Snow, and I will always be here for you. And I just was trying to give you time. But I have wanted you to be my wife for the longest time."

He couldn't take it anymore; he went down on one knee right there in the middle of Fredericksburg. She gasped as he took her hand in his and looked up at her. "Rita Snow, I want to ask you to be my wife. Will you marry me?"

Her eyes filled with tears and she laughed. "I will. I didn't think you were ever going to ask." And then she threw her arms around his neck and sat down on his knee, and he kissed her.

He held her close and kissed her like he had wanted to kiss her from the first moment he had seen her—when he had no right to. When he had been so confused by her, he didn't know how to act considering she had been a wedding crasher—a member of a group he couldn't stand—and yet he couldn't stand not to be near her.

Now, he held her close and felt her heart beating against his, felt her soft lips open to his, and her hands squeezing his shoulders as her arms were wrapped around him. And he was in bliss. If he died there and went to heaven, everything was worth it. Except he didn't want that to happen; he wanted to live a long and happy life with this beautiful woman.

"I think this is going to be a great adventure," he said against her lips.

She nodded and then, without saying anything else, kissed him.

EPILOGUE

They were married. Rita danced in her husband's strong arms as the band played one of the many love songs they'd picked for their wedding reception. Her heart was so full. So very full of love and contentment and excitement about life with Levi.

"I love you," he whispered against her ear and it sent sensations of love and promise coursing through her.

"I love you more," she said, smiling up at him. "I'm so very happy."

"And I'm planning on keeping you that way. I promise from this day forward that's my life's goal."

And she believed him. She'd met a man she could trust with her whole heart. "And I'm going to do the same for you." They smiled at each other and he kissed her lips.

He chuckled as he pulled away and nodded over her shoulder, spinning her so she could see Toby dressed in his western tuxedo jacket and jeans just like Levi's. He had his Stetson on and his fancy boots and he was doing some kind of twist and jig on the dance floor.

"Look, Grandma and Grammy, I'm dancing" He called to his grandmothers, who both stood on the edge of the dance floor beaming as they watched their grandson do his funny dance that went to his own beat despite the one the band was playing.

"You're looking good," her mother called and snapped pictures.

"I see you, sweetie. Smile and let us take your picture," Laura laughed, looking so happy, it touched Rita's heart to see both her mom and Laura looking so good.

Toby did as he was asked; he grinned big and, in the style of a real cowboy, he lifted his little Stetson off his head and waved it in the air.

His grandmothers and others watching laughed and Rita did too, touching her forehead to Levi's when their eyes met. "I am so happy how this turned out."

"Me too, darlin'."

A month ago, after she and Levi had realized their love for each other she had taken Levi with her to go pick up Toby from Laura's. They had sat down and they had an open discussion about her and Levi's plans to get married and that she was always going to be able to provide for him, that her business was doing great and that they wanted her to be in Toby's life. Laura was welcome to visit the ranch at any time and stay—there was plenty of room. She was welcome to come for holidays, and Toby would be always welcome to go with Laura when she scheduled it with Rita and it worked with her schedule.

To Rita's relief, Laura had agreed. She had been concerned by the rumors her former boss—a family friend—had spread about her. But she'd found out the rumors were untrue, and was relieved and was no longer friends with Rita's ex-boss. Laura was happy for Rita and Levi and their love and had also confessed that Toby had talked nonstop about Levi. It had been very clear to her that he loved Levi and that Levi had been a very good influence on Toby. Now, watching them, Rita's heart was so full at how everything had turned out.

She and Levi had set their wedding date quickly, knowing they wanted to be a family now, and Laura and her mother had come to stay at the ranch and to help each other watch Toby while she and Levi were on their honeymoon. Jake was planning to come over several times to give Toby riding lessons on Rosey. The horse was doing great, getting healtier month by month and totally crazy about Toby, who was just as crazy about the horse. Everything was working out perfectly.

As the song ended and the DJ announced that it was time for the garter toss and for all the single men to gather round, Rita was thinking about all that had happened in the last few months leading up to this beautiful night. She could not state enough her happiness. She thanked the Lord for leading her here to Levi. She'd made a very bad move on her part—trying to sell someone's private pictures, of all things—but leave it to God; He had turned a bad situation into a good situation, the best situation—and she had met the love of her life. And that just filled her heart and made her want to shout from the rooftops.

Levi lifted his gaze from watching Toby wave his hat for his grandmas and when Levi's eyes touched hers, a thrill raced through her. It never ceased to warm her heart how connected they were.

"I love how happy they all are," Levi said. "Same as me." He grinned. "Now, I get to take that garter off that lovely leg of yours and send it sailing to some lucky guy. I'd never in a million years guessed how amazing catching the one at Cole's wedding was going to change my life."

She chuckled. "Are you sure it was catching the garter? You were coming after me and my camera long before you caught that garter."

He laughed. "True. But who knows, all this might not have turned out the same way if I hadn't caught it. Cole swears that catching a garter changed his life for the better and I'm now agreeing with him."

"And I'm not going to disagree. I'm anxious to see who the lucky fella is. Who knows, maybe the one who catches your garter will fall in love with Hanna, the vet, since she caught my bouquet."

"Maybe, you never know. Hey, Jake, don't you go sneaking off. Get in line with Bret and all the other lonely bachelors. This could be your lucky day."

Jake gave Levi a teasing frown. "I am not the marrying kind, but I'll get in your lineup if it makes you happy."

"It does, and Bret, you get in there too, brother."

Bret just laughed and stepped into the group. "Only for you, little brother, on your special day."

When Jake said he wasn't the marrying kind, he was right from everything Rita had observed. She adored Jake but he dated often from what she'd seen and no one steadily. He loved to have a good time and especially loved dancing. She believed he'd probably danced with every single female in the room. Well, not Hanna, the vet, as the two did not seem particularly fond of each other.

And then there was Bret, the cowboy had no time

for love, only his love of rodeo. She'd only been around him a few times and she liked him. Liked him a lot, he was nice, dedicated to his career and had been super with Toby. But like Jake, he did not seem to be the marrying kind at this point in his career. But he loved his family and she liked how to please Levi on his wedding day he joined in the fun.

Rita sat down in the chair and Levi knelt on one knee as everyone watched and pictures were taken, as far as she knew all were legitimate pictures since Levi had tried extra, extra hard to have no paparats here.

Levi looked up at her and winked as she slipped her foot from her shoe and exposed just enough of her leg for him to tug the garter down and slip it over her ankle then her foot. Grinning, he stood waved it at the guys then turned his back on them.

"Get ready, fellas, one of you boys is about to have a life-changing event happen when you catch this pretty strip of lace."

She watched all the gleeful grins and good-natured elbowing as the fellas jostled for a front row position. Neither of Levi's single brothers stepped up to the plate. She laughed at their antics to get to the back of the pack.

"Heads up here it comes," Levi hollered and flung the garter over his head with the force of a professional baseball pitcher.

She watched as the white garter flew straight through the mass of guys who were jumping, shoving, and tripping each other as they tried to reach it. But like it was meant to be, it was as if in all of their antics they parted, and the garter sailed straight at a startled Bret. At the last minute the professional bull rider lifted his hands and caught the garter, his mouth fell open and his eyes widened. And then he laughed and held it up in the air.

"Ha," Levi whooped when he turned and saw him. "This should be good. Real good." And then he took her hands and tugged her into his arms. "Now, we've got that situation started let's get back to you and me and getting that cake cut then we're heading to the plane and getting this honeymoon started. I'm ready to start our life together."

"I agree wholeheartedly." Then hand in hand they went in search of a cake.

* * *

Don't miss the next book in the series: Billionaire Cowboy's Hill Country Proposal as Bret Tanner finds out that what his brother's suspect is true: when a Tanner brother catches a garter, it means true love is about to happen.

A second chance romance about a billionaire bull rider and the girl he left behind. Rumors and secrets can tear a relationship apart, but can the truth mend broken hearts or is it too late for love?

Bull riding champion Bret Tanner is home to help with a family charity event, but when Ellie Seton shows up asking for an interview, he has no plans to open up to the woman who broke his heart years ago.

Ellie is desperate for the interview and not thrilled about having to convince Bret to talk to her. He broke her heart when he chose bull riding and a tabloid worthy lifestyle over her. Now, she's an entertainment columnist and needs this interview or she'll lose her job. When her mother, the town florist, is injured, Ellie must step in to help fulfill the flower orders for the Tanner family's charity event.

Can Ellie use helping with the event to get the interview she needs? Or will working side by side with Bret be too much for her heart to bear?

Also from Hope Moore

Thank you for reading! Want to be the first to know about exclusive promotions, news, giveaways and new releases? Sign up for my newsletter here: www.subscribepage.com/hopemooresignup

Reviews help other readers find new books. I always appreciate when my readers take time to leave and honest review. It is so helpful to me!

I love hearing from my readers. Please feel free to contact me at authorhopemoore@gmail.com

About the Author

Hope Moore is the pen name of an award-winning author who lives deep in the heart of Texas surrounded by Christian cowboys who give her inspiration for all of her inspirational sweet romances. She loves writing clean & wholesome, swoon worthy romances for all of her fans to enjoy and share with everyone. Her heartwarming, feel good romances are full of humor and heart, and gorgeous cowboys and heroes to love. And the spunky women they fall in love with and live happily-ever-after.

When she isn't writing, she's trying very hard not to cook, since she could live on peanut butter sandwiches, shredded wheat, coffee...and cheesecake why should she cook? She loves writing though and creating new stories is her passion. Though she does love shoes, she's admitted she has an addiction and tries really hard to stay out of shoe stores. She, however, is not addicted to social media and chooses to write instead of surf FB - but she LOVES her readers so she's working on a free novella just for you and if you sign up for her newsletter she will send it to you as soon as its ready! You'll also receive snippets of her adventures, along with special deals, sneak peaks of soon-to-be released books and of course any sales she might be having.

She promises she will not spam you, she hates to be spammed also, so she wouldn't dare do that to people she's crazy about (that means YOU). You can unsubscribe at any time.

Sign up for my newsletter:
www.subscribepage.com/hopemooresignup

I can't wait to hear from you.

Hope Moore~
Always hoping for more love, laughter and reading for you every day of your life!

www.ingramcontent.com/pod-product-compliance
Lightning Source LLC
Chambersburg PA
CBHW070622100726
47907CB00007B/1832